For Celia
& Marguerite
with affection

Thomas
&
Karen

'86

For outsiders like me, who have sometimes managed a glimpse of contemporary Dutch poetry, Schierbeek has long appeared as the dominant figure, energetic and graceful over forty years or more. This poem-novel goes beyond anything we've seen, to place him among the masters of an art that breaks distinctions between genres.

Jerome Rothenberg

K a t y d i d   B o o k s

TRANSLATIONS
General Editor, Thomas Fitzsimmons

ASIAN POETRY

Japan:

Devil's Wind: A Thousand Steps, by Yoshimasu Gôzô

Sun, Sand and Wind, by Shozu Ben

A String Around Autumn: Selected Poems 1952-1980, by Ōoka Makoto

Treelike: The Poetry of Kinoshita Yûji

Dead Languages: Selected Poems 1946-1984, by Tamura Ryûichi

Celebration in Darkness: Selected Poems of Yoshioka Minoru; &
Strangers' Sky: selected Poems of Iijima Kôichi

A Play of Mirrors: Eight Major Poets of Modern Japan, edited by Ōoka Makoto
and Thomas Fitzsimmons

A Thousand Steps . . . and More: Selected Poems and Prose 1964-1984, by
Yoshimasu Gôzô

EUROPEAN WRITING

The Netherlands:

Cross Roads -- a 'Compositional Novel' by Bert Schierbeek

Cross Roads

European Writing in Translation
The Netherlands #1

Cross Roads

Bert Schierbeek

*Translated
by*

Charles McGeehan

KATYDID BOOKS
Oakland University
Rochester MI
1988

Produced by K T DID Productions

Originally published as *Betrekkingen* by
DE BEZIGE BIJ, Amsterdam, 1979

FIRST AMERICAN EDITION 1988

Supported by the Foundation for the Promotion of the Translation of
Dutch Literary Works

*Book Design, Cover and Illustrations by
Karen Hargreaves-Fitzsimmons*

Printed on acid free paper by Thomson-Shore, Michigan, USA

Library of Congress Cataloging-in-Publication Data

Schierbeek, Bert, 1918-
    Cross roads.

        (European writing in translation. The Netherlands ; #1)
        Translation of: Betrekkingen.
        I. Title. II. Series.
        PT5868.S28B4813 1988   839.3'1364   87-22722
        ISBN 0-942668-11-1 (alk. paper)

Contents

for Thea

Introduction

Bert Schierbeek is one of the most significant writers of his generation and it is only the accident of his language being Dutch that has kept him from most people's notice for so long.

Called up during the Second World War, he escaped after surrender in 1940 to fight in the Dutch Resistance. His experiences then provided the material for the two conventional novels with which he began his writing career shortly after the war. He found his true voice at the beginning of the '50s when he began writing what have been termed his "compositional novels." In these, Schierbeek's theoretical point of departure is that a life-like presentation of the facts in fiction is itself fiction. Real life consists of many unrelated events coexisting side by side, interconnections between which can be seen by intuitional leaps; so the novel should not falsify by linear progression and the overstructuring of reality. Although he may owe something to such writers as Joyce, Pound and, later on, Olson, he created a totally new form in which prose and verse reinforce each other in providing "cross sections of reality." His attitude toward language is that all spoken and written vocabularies should be put to use in such a way that the conceptual unit of the word is freed into new and more significant areas of apprehension. In one of his essays on the creative process he passes from the scientific postulation that all matter is energy in motion to the prediction that "great rhythmic unities are going to replace the story, the novel." The compositional novel is an energy construct of welded information providing a cross-sectional view of all existence in which the eye/ego is only a part of many. It is a shifting stream of inspiration and in-formation, possessing currents and eddies in which is captured the total continuum rather than the small areas to which the normal divided awareness responds. Thus the consciousness is expanded to see how part goes with whole, how "I" and other are one.

Schierbeek's first three books in the new style, *Het boek ik* (The Book I, 1951), *De andere namen* (The Other Names, 1952) and *De derde persoon* (The Third Person, 1955) are roughly autobiographical in nature. They set out to demonstrate by their layered and allusive texture the oneness of personal experience and human history. As Schierbeek comments on the first of the novels, "the book is actually about the removal of the borderlines of the "I" and their redistribution".

So far as one can judge from the excerpts in Charles McGeehan's anthology *Shapes of the Voice* (Boston, 1977), there appears to be a balance between verse and prose in this trilogy -- to speak of the form: in essence they are pure poetry, language heightened to an extraordinary density of significance. In the books that followed the verse form comes to predominate. *De gestalte der stem* (The Shape of the Voice, 1957), *Het dier heeft een mens getekend* (The Beast Drawn Man, 1960) and *Ezel mijn bewoner* (Donkey my Inhabitant, 1964) also form a trilogy. This time the oneness of consciousness is explored by way of the mental processes. Schierbeek draws on myth to provide the framework about which the mosaic of personal experience grows. This has to be expressed in language (which is the point of the title *The Shape of the Voice*) in a manner

14

similar to the cosmic process. Out of the void comes form, out of empty breath the fullness of words; the laws by which they are governed are like.

One impetus towards Schierbeek's search for a new form was his membership of the COBRA group of experimental artists and writers whose ideology approximated that of the American Abstract Expressionists and the "New York School" of writers connected with them. Renewal of means was sought in the semiautomatic gesture which was consciously interpreted only after completed. In this way the old boundaries and concepts of form circumscribing the arts were broken so that the various disciplines came together on common ground and reinforced each other. In American literature the process was more advanced than in Europe and we find Schierbeek's work overlapping several important developments there. His first trilogy was written between the appearance of Pound's *Pisan Cantos* (1948) and the "Rockdrill" section (1955); the publication of the first novel in the series coincided with that of the last book of William's original *Patterson*. Meanwhile Olson's *Maximus* poems were appearing in limited editions from Stuttgart (1953-6). Nineteen fifty-nine, when Schierbeek was well into his second trilogy, saw the publication of Pound's *Thrones* cantos, Olson's essay on projective verse, and the dislocations of Burroughs' *The Naked Lunch* (Paris edition). Schierbeek was later to consider all these writers in his critical work *Een broek voor een oktopus* (Pants for an Octopus, 1964). In addition, his method is prefigured in Wallace Stevens' "Notes Towards a Supreme Fiction." His subject is abstract in that it is not to be captured in, but divined through language

15

rhythmically ordered in a new way. This rhythm matches the fluency of life as a whole, where all is in touch with all. Language's tendency to isolate and arrest the process by naming distorts reality. During the new fiction's progress, however, the significance of things is seen to change. Pleasure arises from the writing's inclusiveness and mimetic nature.

When Rimbaud spoke of the need for a new mythology he was asking that man give up his conventional ways of viewing himself, and launch on a voyage of discovery with no landmarks to guide him. It was to this end that the artistic means were to be renewed. The function of myth is to explain in a graphic way the impact of the outside world upon the individual, to dramatise the inward process of apprehending. This also is the task of language which equally has no link with reality other than through the mental processes of those who use it. The behavior of language itself in its pure form, stripped of our habitual and private associations, might therefore be the very stuff of the new mythology. Something of this is explored in the collage of quotation, conversation and anthropological fact in *Een grote dorst* (A Great Thirst, 1968) and *Inspraak* (Speak-in, 1970). Schierbeek's approach here is that since each personality's world-view is a result of verbal input, it is a kind of paradigm of all others. As personal and universal history coalesce in his first trilogy, so the experience of our linguistic inheritance is now seen to be one. Our mode of expression is made up of fragments of all other expressions, just as the compositional novel attempts to hold in supension the sum of universal experience.

In the '70s Schierbeek turned to writing poems of small compass, exploring the possibilities of what can be said in restricted forms. Some of these consist of slowly building and transforming word patterns, in the manner of his Belgian contemporary, the Constructivist writer Mark Insiel. Others have the dense and elusive logic of Robert Creeley's later work. He goes on to a consideration of conceptual and other mental structures, memory, imagination, dream. Gradually the pieces get longer and his next extended theme emerges. Whereas earlier he had investigated internal structures, now he followed the external information through its internal transformations in order to establish some relations between such dissimilar entities. Both in the poem *Mexico 1*, which forms part of the volume *Vallen en opstaan* (Falling & Standing Up, 1977), and in *Weerwerk* (Keeping it up, 1977), he quotes Merleau-Ponty's "Consciousness is a function of the body, it is therefore an 'event' within the body dependent on the events outside" as an indicator of the way his interest is turning.

His works become demonstrations of how, in the words of his great Flemish experimental predecessor Paul van Ostayen (1896-1928), "the phenomena of the physical world are stored in the subconscious, where they interpenetrate and act upon one another."

Keeping it Up is the first work of Schierbeek's latest trilogy and a continuation of his overall theme of "The shape of the voice," which again makes use of autobiographical material. For Schierbeek, the surface structure of linear narrative hides the deeper pattern of interconnections between words and people, their interdependence. Not to take these into account leaves a void at the center of meaning. Communication resembles the heterogeneous sets of china he mentions, left after so many items have been broken, and must be so approached as to give a sense of all the missing pieces.

Individual interpretation is only one among a multitude of possible structures. For "reality" to emerge there must be a synthesis of all. Hence the form in which "prose and verse cross-fertilize each other." It is a slow unfolding of grammatical units and small images which modify each other as the work develops. Where *Keeping it Up* concentrates more upon the barriers we erect and the suffering that the consequent ignorance entails, the next novel, *Betrekkingen* (Cross Roads), considers the overleaping of these barriers. The dominating image here is the new sense of richness Eulalia gains from being taught to read. The theme of personal interdependence is stressed far more. We have no meaningful existence outside of others (just as language is an enclosed and self-defining system); violence and unlove at any point disjoints the whole.

That the very concept of "self" and "other" is just such a violence Schierbeek sets out to demonstrate and heal in his writing. His method is that of collage whereby entities, events, and memories, seemingly discrete in themselves, come together in a pattern greater and more significant than the sum of the parts. Voice and image build up a web of cross-reference which grows in complexity with repetition and addition until insight rises out of their mingling. Schierbeek has given as his reason for abandoning conventional narrative that "life is 777 stories at the same time," and again, "everthing coheres with everything else. I see coherence of structures in layers." He may have been influenced by the visionary abstract painter Wols (1913-51) who had written

> the elusive penetrates everything
> you must know that everything rhymes

Wols used a collage technique to demonstrate this in his own writing. Schierbeek's is very similar. He writes down significant images, thoughts, scraps of conversation, on pieces of paper until there emerges for him the way into a new work. Then he assembles these collage materials and allows his mind to play over them until connections form and the work grows of itself. All he has to do is follow the mind at its work, to relinquish control once he has done the basic work of gathering, and see where he is taken.

Something of this is acknowledged in the subtitle of *A Great Thirst*: A Chain Reaction. Or as Olson has expressed it, "one perception grows immediately out of another." It is obvious that this way he will reproduce not the falsifying finished product of traditional art but the process of the mind before it is so formed. The senses feed the mind with a disparate stream of different impressions, from which it selects what seem most significant and establishes connections between them. The process is known as syntax, it is what we do when we choose from the total field of language. And again, it is how we react in the presence of Lautréamont's "fortuitous meeting on an operating table of a sewing machine and an umbrella." We explain the presence of these disparate elements to ourselves, we draw them together in a common association. This is the work of the metaphorical process.

Schierbeek, then, is pioneering in the unified field of scientist and mystic, he is demonstrating by his work the irrefutable links between macrocosm and microcosm. In addition there arises a political lesson of which he is also well aware. If there is this oneness of experience, then any man who attempts to deprive another of his own sense of it, by imposing on him a personal view or will alien to his own, commits the height of insolense. He is impious, he blasphemes against the truth. The aesthetic corollary hardly needs pointing out. What follows, as in all Schierbeek's writing, is a text which is only incomplete and disjointed until you too have entered it.

Yann Lovelock
Birmingham
England

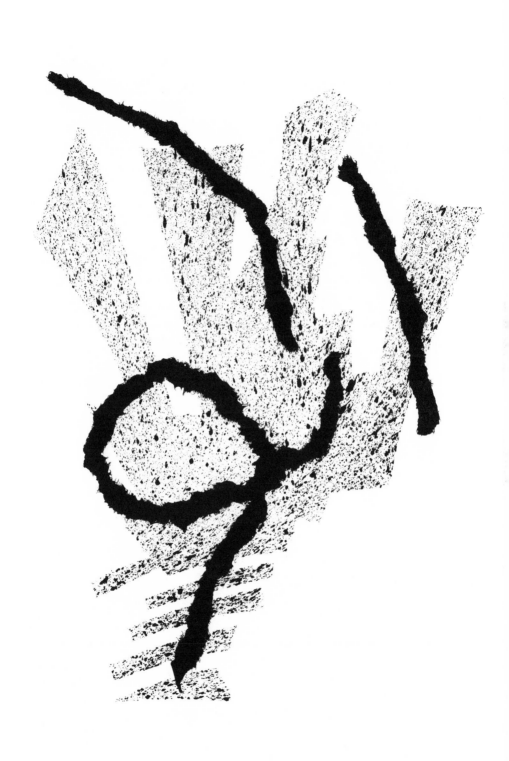

Cross Roads

even we
maybe
have nothing
in common
only maybe
said he
that our breaths
cross each other
and we owing to
the odor which we have
in common
(and enhanced into fragrance)
quickly round the corner

for someone builds a stairway
and someone else
kicks you up- or down-
        stairs
my eyes
said Craig Strete*
see through the spheres

of pain
said he
maybe it is no more
than a relation
for instance
that dreaming is looking
into the night
to see things
and that they start speaking
what you see
but just awake
can barely put into words
like now on my birthday
that is always tomorrow
or yesterday
whereupon I go into the time
of my birth
ever again
and am ready
ever again
and so-equipped as well

whereupon someone will always call out
as long as it's a good relationship
(and brings something in as well)

> *now and then too said he*
> *since I can see traces*
> *passes slowly through*

the leaves before
my eyes
the form of a hand

a ship sails
through the cactuses
very slowly
no ship

"out of the terrible visions
of yesterday we come back"
knowing the nothing of the cat
that plays with nothing

a lot of sleep said Mingus
with one eye closed said he
I try to play
my truth
to play what I am
and the hard thing about it
comes from the fact that I myself
am constantly changing
anyhow
it keeps you going

maybe you think
that's how you overcome
space by yourself
becoming space

then too
that lovely one
that last one
who so much wanted to go further
and worked because working this
dear one thought brought you further
that was the idea

and yet before her time

sometimes it's hard
and always
the gums
uphill
downhill

no
we don't want to know of any
names anymore
for rightly so
the word sometimes
withdraws into itself
and gives nothing away

as Marcel said:

       you stand there staring
       at the stars
       and there they are again

o no
whispers
(who?)
> *you have*
> *nothing to fear*
> *here comes no-one back*

you
withdraw
now only voice
the voice withdraws
now only word
the word withdraws
now only silence
both withdraw
silence
now only voice

as they say:

> Antonio's a wonderful storyteller
> because they're never written down

it's true
before you know it
something you don't know about
is running around on its own
out of hand
you can't wash them
anymore
> all clean

you think o god
whoever forgets
one hand the other
one too

since new insights
come when the night still
isn't quite sleep
nor really awake

so you're blind
your face is covered as well
and the distance
yet not shortsighted
when the distance is well known

more or less
the snail of your self
the house on your back

so never at home

tho often unexpectedly
land in a completely
made bed
that is indeed made
completely

you're lying down at home
flat on your back
beside yourself
says William Klein
(photographer)
what I'd find the greatest thing
     he's sitting thinking
     upon a rock
     a very cool one
     in his eyes a ship
     white in the distance
     in the midst of Manhattan
says he
they don't come by anymore
but the greatest thing would be:
              to make photographs
              just as incomprehensible
              as life
that would be
the greatest if it could be done
but the ships go to Newark and Hoboken
so you unbolt yourself
and you forget it
as well as what flew up
a bird
a crossing
meanwhile
your hair was getting
in your hands when

Jan Hendriksen called out
(thirteen TVs on the wall
and all of them on)
aren't they beautiful
almost like the old days
(and all of 'em the same)
says Bernie
(Bernie Bishop)
for a moment
steering with one hand melted
(almost)
you spin the wheel around
(the chocolate's also melted)
and then
it's all at a standstill
a while later
all loaded up
(caviar)
across those waters
all along the edge
of darkness
for a moment
light

no-one sees it

no
still on the road
to Jericho

on the gums
uphill downhill
                seven camels
                on one rope
                along the horizon
                on the road to Jericho
                with one man
                alone
and born alone for sure
with so many others
and with us
and those animals
and even yet
with so many and the animals
naked upon the land

the boundaries of man become as my friend said
obliterated the moment they reach the infinite
and that happens every day

Thea gives lessons to Eulalia*
who cannot read or write
lessons in reading and writing
and now she reads
mi pa-pa fu-ma una pi-pa
and then quickly follows
mi papa fuma una pi-pa
sounds and images come together
in a sentence she already knew

she gets touched by the infinite
in great wonderment

her husband José who *can* read
and write says
(as to the drawing up of a will)
you've got to arrange for that properly
(write it out, as he said)
since in the lives of the parents
children are mainly good friends
but when there is something to inherit
that often proves disappointing
and I think too that he thinks
what if Eulalia can read and
write and gets touched
by the infinite. . .
no one sees it
still on the way
thus it comes closer
and in between
the terror
closer than the skirt

Eulalia however says after the lesson
for me it is still always
easier to plant the vine
than to read and write

          meanwhile: they're standing there again
                       like they'd stood there
                       (at Waterloo, one thought)
                       in battle array
                       by the thousands
                       and suddenly a little whistle
                       (somebody blew a whistle)
                       and it began
                       begins it
                       hurrah.

flies over
all those names
of the nameless
who're lying there

                       naturally we
                       for example let
                       the sample in between
                       for example
                       for what it was

all filled up
with this love this
uttermost until the last
gasp keeps on working
because you would take it
further and true to duty
until the end that never

was in sight
later you hear:

        if you want to get up onto the roof
        do use a ladder

writes my father:

        time flies past, the vacations are over,
        back to work again the ice still hasn't
        melted but the world will get caught in
        the clutches of money, power and luxury
        again. Again some difficult issues will
        have to be worked out. A grasp of one
        another's viewpoints is far off. The Pope
        is dead. Who will his successor be.

I speak with him later:

        yes I did have the grip and haven't been
        outside in three weeks it was so slippery
        and also have a bandage around my leg,
        but I don't lose heart. . . and do the
        therapeutic exercises with vigor.
he becomes 90

and then I think of Zoetemelk
(the racing cyclist) who could never
ride out of his own shadow

they're standing in battle array again
there's always that little whistle

sure:

       it runs ahead of us
       that mighty model of
       hearing audience obedience
       through all those days
       of the innocent children
       on the edge of the knife
       the last breath of terror
       where the infinite threatens
       the end they didn't ask for
       and one doesn't ask for
       divided up in time
       there's always time
       no mirror in which one can
       recognize himself better than when
       trying to get the hang of a hangover

o and dying
he was singing:

       how bright is
       light actually
       a super black
       hole

so we go on a trip
with a day in staves
and still one spot
where it doesn't leak

said mother Cosme:

        it has changed so

        and improved at that

so now I sit before my house

and the whole world comes past

years ago I'd sit here too

tho you wouldn't really see anything

but the same old stuff

yet I did see

the stars at night and saw

them so shot and the bears

had shifted so much

that we after so many years

would hardly be able to recognize

ourselves in that shift anymore

maybe because it goes

so slowly. . .

in the prolongation of your own shadow

for Craig said:

       visions

       come over you

       when the night still

       isn't quite sleep

       or the dream of

       before the awakening

       stirs and

       gives away

Catalina however
of the Fonda
of Pepe
(who built it all with his own hands)
says
very slowly
(her words drawn out
of her deepest Moorish grounds
unbeknownst to herself)
says she
as languid in speech as her
gestures her walk and look
(and yet seeing all)
says she
what Julian her son
(her only child)
has already said
(two days before)
that they both
(his parents)
Catalina and Pepe
surely wanted to take a trip
a big one to South America
there they have relatives
says Catalina
because we have relatives there
in Buenos Aires and we also speak
the language we should be able to go
since they too had once been here

that is a nephew and a niece
a son and a daughter of one of
Pepe's brothers
so it's simple
(tenemos casa)
we needn't drop it as far as money goes
so we should be able to go
as Julian says
for the first time they'd be going on a trip
(farther than Barcelona)
and it's about time they go
they've done nothing but work all the time
and have thought a lot about money
so says Catalina
we should actually be able to go
but the trouble is just this
Pepe won't fly
and I wouldn't go by boat for my life
so said she
we really won't get there together
and we don't want to go separately either
so we won't ever get there

I think about birds
about Marcel* and Meneer de Ruiter
(both equally bald)
Mr. de Ruiter
Mr. Hart de Ruiter of Natural History
(he also loved birds and the mystery

of flying)
the mystery of flying is
to Marcel merely a
tap against the air
said Meneer de Ruiter:

> when these
> migratory birds leave
> they always go together
> never alone
> alone is death

(said Marcel):

> they're gathering
> you can hear them
> how they're going to do it
> this time I think
> and about the weather

Meneer de Ruiter:

> they don't choose a direction
> they've got no choice
> they go where they've got to
> to survive and to
> propagate themselves
> they've got more brains
> in their tail than in
> their head

thinks Marcel:

> even a bird is *one*
> and indivisible

(he sees it
but doesn't say so
Marcel)
Meneer de Ruiter:

> on the way they always stop
> at the same places
> seldom at others
> only out of dire necessity
> and they do know of that too
> built-in radar
> no room for play
> that's the difference between
> a bird and a human being

says Julian later
that he thinks they
are not going to go

Marcel however
his large head
full of uncomprehended dreams
says: sometimes I think that

> they know of a beginning
> tho not an end
> that life is
> maybe a phase
> something like
> becoming a cloud
> we people and birds

Catalina looks at her son
and isn't going to tell him
never that when he was due to
be born and didn't want to be
the old pastor had to come by
with three big black pigs
to cast him out of her

and perhaps she thinks
that's why he keeps on
mucking around
that apple of her eye

for Julian the question remains
does he or doesn't he muck around
says Annette from Düsseldorf:

> *man weisz es ja nicht*
> *nicht sicher*
> *aber doch sagt man*
> *bei uns:*
> *"Das leben ist ein Kinderhemd*
> *kurz und beschissen"**

Meneer de Ruiter however
(he's standing very erect
his bald head in unprece-
dented airs)
says:

41

look
that birds can fly
we do know
and why they can fly
too
they've got wings
but
how they fly
we do not know
that is we don't know
how that weft of feathers
works when a bird
flies

later on behind the bar
(where one now seldom finds him)
claims Pepe that he'd really like to fly
and that he also knows that many people do it
but that even so he wouldn't dare to and
claims he besides here I really have
all I need my house the café
the pensión the restaurant
and built it all with my own hands

those who now fly here
have a house here
that they haven't built themselves
but yet a house

(a little later)
whereas actually I'm a fisherman
many water closets were also wrongly placed
and also the discharge
what did we know about discharge
we'd crap among the cactuses
and always a stone
to wipe your arse
in the civil war my uncle was
shot dead because he was for
the government
thus a republican
and they said he was a communist
and we didn't even know
who our government was
this island didn't exist
in Madrid

thereafter
he can see
in fact there's not one square meter
left
full up
he sighs: all those beds

Meneer de Ruiter however
cried out:
        intolerable differences
        between Nature and ourselves

we will abolish
we have built imitation birds
and can also fly
for tho born with leaden feet
we do have a head
full of birds

and for a moment we thought:
(he raised his hands)

        damn we thought
        he sees them flying
        (he himself flying out)
        out of his bald head
        (just wore out his third wife too)
        we saw them flying
        his arms raised up
        (conjurative wingbeat)

and he cried out
real loud
(like on the cross):

        and all of you
        and all those lessons
        the whole "soggy saga"
        the complete natural history
        resides in you all

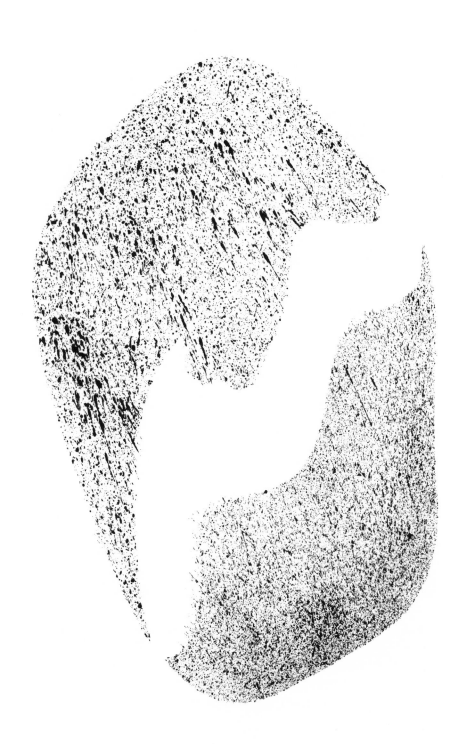

from the first cell to the latest
the complete cosmogenesis
from the first nebula
the first star
to the animal that crawled out of
the sea onto the land and
had to develop lungs and a nose
for breathing upon earth and
feet for walking upon it
being transferred from cell to cell
the composition of it all
internally provided-for

: centuries of programming
of interrelations
(the eye with which I see you
we can see with the eye with which
you see me)
relationships
involvements
arrangements
for survival
(*moraleinfrei*)*

unforgettable
for a moment I thought
Raskolnikov
and for lack of

anything better
to do he beats
himself up
but no
his arms dropped
so did his voice
he said:
>better go now
>the hour is up
(he did rub the sweat
off of his bald head)

says Eulalia
for the first time writing
her own name:
>*Eulalia Ramòn Juan*
(very slowly)
(quite precisely)
says she:
>I think that I have lived
>in many worlds
>and that this one might just
>turn out to be the most beautiful
>altho first there's a lot of
>work in the field with the trees
>the plants the animals the birds
>and more later on the farm
>and always going to fetch water
>making shoes knitting shirts and

always doing the wash
and later on that horrible aunt
but now
now I can read and write
what earlier on I could only
hear
I lived
(altho not unhappily)
only by
hearsay

says her daughter
now you do have to buy glasses
otherwise you'll be blind by the time
that you can read

so then you take off
the cats have gobbled up
the cheese
you take off
conjurative wingbeat
hobbling
into space

Pepe got a postcard
from California with a real
swimming pool on it
he got it from Bernie Bishop
from New York on vacation in California

wrote Bernie:

>Pepe here it's just like Formentera
>but with more houses people and
>swimming pools

Pepe took a good look
at that picture postcard
(still dreaming of fish
fish for breakfast over
a low fire on the beach)
says he later:

>I had a look at this postcard
>saw this piscina and thought
>I can do that too
>and I'll use it as a model

Marcel too
(suddenly)
chooses the unknown
a blushing woman from
La Sablonière who laughs a lot
wherein all dreams birds and all
of Germany comes to a halt
(his car he does not park
in front of her house)

and later on I heard
of the "greenhouse effect"
a sort of haze never known before
that we ourselves make

totally man-made
but that envelopes us
smothers us more rapidly
than Nature
until the waters rise once more
the poles melt
and the earth. . .

> *but friends*
> *time knows*
> *of no time*
> *stands still*
> *pinches itself*
> *to pieces*
> *cannot stand*
> *eternity*
>
> *eternity knows*
> *of no time*

Pepe looks
at the superb oval
on the picture postcard and thinks
(with plenty of fish
and distance still in his eyes
as well as the wind. . .)
"swimming pool"
a finely formed kidneybean oval
he drew a copy of it
a year later in the void

(in much less than San Francisco de California)
a swimming pool
with a discharge three hundred meters long
to the pulses, tomatoes, cebollas and patatas
(plus a fully electric filter)
and surrounded with trees an outdoor café
with sun umbrellas tables reclining deckchairs
customers and a bar
and behind it Catalina
(*no hay deprisa*)

plenty of time in a smile of centuries
which file past more slowly by the hour
and give her an indelible figure
(as well one which gives and takes)
a smile which somehow sometimes
would make the Buddha envious
(if he didn't know better)

> *you see the moon*
> *and the clouds that*
> *surround it at a total*
> *standstill*
>
> *(for just a moment)*
> *but there in the*
> *shoulders of*
> *some of us it*
> *comes for a moment*

52

to a standstill
bent there into
an ache
that up there
(you should know)
and you do know

. . .

but no
hoho
here right on the border
between San Fernando and Es Caló*
ohoh
CO
COtwo
(a greenhouse of course)
and the effect

the way he walked Chagall
(of course there's that way of the Cross)
across the terrace frontage of
Mishkenot Sha'ananim
(peaceful dwelling)
he walked an other way
in a gray jacket
across an othergray pair of pants
(he is small)
his eyes too
two fluttering birds
well-trained carbuncles

(two lovers nevertheless
a bit worn-out above Witebsk)
he walked
very calmly over to Teddy
Teddy Kollek
(mayor of Jerusalem)
came to pick him up
two birds arm in arm
over to the Israel Museum
opposite the Knesset
where just now Sadat
gives Golda Meir a kiss
and she for him a little present
for his grandson

       people cried out rejoicing
       it's beyond
       comprehension
       and instinct

so together
Chagall and Kollek
on the steps of
the Israel Museum
(all of it in the shadow
of Sandberg*
who cast it)
       no not to the Wailing Wall
       not there where so many

kisses go up in centuries
of smoke. . .

says Kollek:
maybe
the dilution
of religion signifies
the beginning of a
conviction for instance
of peace between Jews
and Arabs and all
who live inside this old city
which as it has been written
was once entirely gilded
a heart of gold
on the inside and outside
a star
then too:
if a star falls make sure
your roof doesn't leak

you see that spot
on Sadat's forehead
every kiss gets melted
and the believers are shaky
their gods asleep

says Mr. Brunn
don't believe any of that

about peace they want to
drive us into the sea
that's all

shouts Meneer Visser
(Mathematics)
even then:
>look
>first I come
>then for quite some time nothing comes
>then comes a load of road apples
>then again for quite some time nothing comes
>and then
>only then do you people come

wrote Abram Terts
(Andrei Sinyavsky)
"And what if you were to create a language of your-own
and were living in it like a monkey in the jungle"
ultimately:
>in every slogan
>lodges a horny ape
>that screws
>you
yet later:
>on David Street
>a golden fan
>hand-hammered
>in Persia

flutters motionless
between two breasts
a shaft of light
flashes into the Souk
and onto the flanks
of the mountains

it is written
Sunday, 6 November 1977
went to Hadassah Synagogue
with the stained-glass windows
of Chagall
and then we had fish

writes Terts
(after so many chilly camp years)
    cosiness and warmth produce
    new thoughts
    and ravens squawk as they do
    because they feel too black
    in all that white snow

I come across Anna Marie in the fonda
she looks through the mail and I ask
did you see any mail for me
said she curtly I don't know
take a look yourself and then shows
a letter to Pep Carnet and
says it's for both of us

because that man makes such bad
coffee machines

o say I

don't forget that I live in Mario's
house and even though he's dead now
that makes little difference
I've now got a residence permit
so a sort of identification card
and now I'm only still allowed to go
into San Francisco and San Fernando
and not to take photos anywhere anymore. . .

look says she
what I am really after all is a kind of
womanly Wandering Jew
(with oversized tits, as Mario had said)
and here in the Sun Belt's fringe area
all sorts of things happen
we're situated right in the middle
that's why I walk around an awful lot
in recent days mainly in the dark
to find things out about the surroundings
since without surroundings you're nowhere

and uh. . .
you were in Israel huhm?
now I'll tell you something

those Palestinians are to my mind
the Jews of the Arabs
they don't give a damn about 'em
and apart from that
here it's also going wrong with all that
tourism in the summer
people don't have time anymore
they take a quick picture of a postcard
and away they go again

apart from that
you've got to endure fields-of-force
but then separated from bed and board

it had been our dream
San Carlos de la Rapita
Baños las Delicias
the whole family was sitting
there shucking beans
and we asked about it
and they said
you are of course going to the sea
you will swim and come back
and sure enough
we did swim
and come back
and they came with buckets
of water and said

you go into the shower stall
and we will throw it over your head

sure enough Baños las Delicias

but tourism moneymaking
and nonchalance
intervene for a moment
and it becomes Pompeii
casting a figurine
getting burned and never again
getting up

Byll and I took some photos
and even got some beans

later on:
>a man is digging himself
>into the ground to build
>a well
>and gasping for breath yells
>beans
>and beer

says Terts
a voice out of the chorus
(with thanks)
about fairy tales in Russia
which tell of summer's flowers

and berries and there's always the stove
the fairy tale
says he
gets literally danced out of the stove
also hitches the stove onto the front of its sledge
and glides forth like a wedding procession
Eulalia works hard every day learning
to read and write and to her surprise
can already read the VIM cleanser ad
and what it costs
says she:

    I have lived in many worlds
    first on Ibiza as a child and
    was then named Eulalia Ramòn Juan
    and would have been glad to go to school
    but we were too poor
    then on Formentera with José
    as *majoral* but without reading
    and writing and now in a world
    greater than I had thought
    that is: with reading and writing
    and see Thea in handwriting
    and myself too and later
    everybody and everything

he did walk around again
brittly in grey
and still total
the pants also

still small
complete in himself
Chagall

>   *o those two*
>   *you think then*
>   *who we were*
>   *and still are*
>   *but no longer*
>   *together*
>   *you think then*
>   *gliding and yet*
>   *yet also inspired*
>   *while flying*
>   *in a whole lot of air*
>   *ungrasped*

of course there's
the way of the Cross
and also that silence
a marvelous mist that we
spread out above that marvelous
Earth upon which we live
with a lot of noise
     encapsulate ourselves
     in great names
     and enterprising
Anna Marie cried out
as she put a bunch of bananas

(just purchased)
into the kitchen sink
(she didn't throw 'em)
she cried out
(yet more a whispering)
no-one heard her
nor saw:

    o kis

    kissinger

    don't kiss

    my finger

but sure
my hand upon it
and high up:

        I'm on probation

        and goddammit I'm not scared

        Eternal Life

        isn't all there is, either

a whole slew of Bavarians are
walking around over the way of the Cross
with home-made cross
Bavarian birches
(the crooked ends missing)
fourteen stations
through an overpopulated
ethnology

    and you hear

Eternal One
Eternal One
you see what you're
hearing that Eternal One
those mothers
nearly dead
they're still snapping

only
they're not saying so
those fathers
solid birch
with a stick behind
a door
of nothing

oh no, what you
hear and see:

        Luther, for instance
        better a dead child
        than a disobedient child

Stammheim
well guarded
smothers
the best
that would better
not have been
smothered

64

said that guy
I do live now in a strange house
the oldest one on the island
four hundred years old, for sure
he whispers
built of the bricks of an old monastery
that once stood there
where? I ask
even worse
people die in there
says he

say I: is that so
no says he people die in there
say I: is that so
all the people who live
in there died says he
say I: is that so
sure, a vein of water
over water means bad sleep
say I: is that so
and that last woman
now all hung up on drinking
drinks up the whole house
and says she wants to keep it
say I: is that so
so I think says he
I'll put *my* money into it

but I've *got* no money
say I: is that so
so now the roof leaks
and the walls lean
and rain and wind and the crows. . .
say I: is that so
but if it's all leaning
and falls apart
how's it going to stay up
say I: is that so
thinks he: oh

don't forget says Anna Marie
that the chairperson of the Society
of the Friends of Friendship
my friend Dr. Renata
no, Renato Poolhouse
Bismarckstrasse
(the number's slipped my mind)
(he does love big tits)
is very well disposed to me
(he sublimates everything)
and so I am one of the Cariños
(he's also gay)
so I am one of the favorites

writes Wieslav Kielar
(häftling nr 290)

in Auschwitz:

> I went to bed early
> but not as usual
> I couldn't sleep
> I thought of home
> of the war
> of the gas chambers
> of the carbolic acid
> (deadly injection)
> of the selections
> the liquidations
> and of friends
> who had all died
> friend Waldek was snoring
> awfully and the wooden planks
> of the sick who had to go
> to the toilet were creaking
> and the groaning and coughing
> and gurgling of the dying
> dear god I thought. . .
> for which sins are people suffering
> and suddenly I also thought
> our enemies are also praying
> to the same god
> then I fell asleep

and whether we'll ever
ever yet be allowed

to experience freedom
said he the next
the next the next and
without end the next morning

in August 1939
the mobilization broke out
me gone off to Hoorn
Recrute Battalion of the 19th
nothing to do
lovely summer
no uniforms in supply
(just wear out your own pants first)
no rifles either
and when they came
no bullets
did have to lug an M-20 to Wognum tho
(prehistoric machinegun)
and then being forgotten in Wognum
on the lookout for (you thought)
an imaginary enemy
you're alone in the haystack
with mice and sparrows and an
outlook across all that cabbage
which was filling the fields
too late
back alone with that M-20
in the barracks
(technical school in Hoorn)

"where are you coming from?"
"there's nobody left to speak of
and the cabbage was also wiped out sergeant"
said I
we also had a guy
from the Orient
Van Pollanen, who couldn't
ever sleep, and in the middle
of the night called out:
(he was from a good family
there were no other kinds)
called out:

> my god
> (which one?)
> my god
> how could it be so
> and I still did think
> that in the West
> like they told me
> civilization begins

sure
it was a dream
but Vink never dreamt
Vink wept for three months
day and night he kept calling out
that he couldn't do it
"what can't you do" we asked
after three months said he

"I can't deal with it
can't stand looking at myself
having to take training to
kill one of you"
"one of us?" we asked
and for the first time completely clear
and without tears he said
"who are you all anyway"

it was an educational time
we marched again to Wognum
and we marched back too
except for Vink
"since you can't march on tears"
said the captain

later he was killed on the Grebbeberg*
never had the time to learn to shoot
but Vink
at night
was never quiet
and called out:

>   *and all this*
>   *and you all*
>   *with eyes shut*
>   *in a world with*
>   *eyes shut*

it was obvious to everyone

Vink had problems
"he thinks too much
and doesn't drink at all" said Jan
who later on
(he knew even then)
would become a dentist
(which he did become)
his father came to see him every two
weeks and joined us for a few beers
at the Veemarkt (cattle market) in Hoorn
and lent me the money that my father
saved by not coming to
see me. . .
Jan's father said
that's how one empty hand fills
the other one and no-one notices
anything. . .
that is: the one comes
        the other doesn't

altho Vink
(mostly at night)
a dream perhaps
of a truth that he
saw and couldn't get over:

                        listen
                        you all
                        you all are built up
                        of empty words

which you can't
fill up
you all
through you all
blows the wind
like through a hole

o says Anna Marie
he kisses your fingers
all ten of 'em
I keep calling out
kiss-off finger
sweet seventeen
oh banana I cry out

tho I do know of course
that I'm on probation
and never do wear those blue beads anymore
because I know
they make me *so* radioactive that
they've got to fasten me down jesus
in iron chains
but even so
Marlène
mit den schönen beinen
*ist meine beste freundin**
I also walk with her through the fields
and with all the dogs on this island
I sow a new field of force

and all those Moorish towers
become storms

she hums:
> *stürme*
> *wie die stürmer*
> *wie hitler*
> *und himmler*
> *stürmen wir*
> *los**

oh
said she
(throwing the bananas
into the sink again)
he kissed my fingers
all ten of 'em
yet during that night
after Vink's word
Van Pollanen keeled over
probably Orientally inspired
and sure enough
the next day Van Pollanen
the Indo (Eurasian) left
perhaps on the power of tea
and his father's palace
but his eyes
I'm sure about this
were utterly full

of rice paddies and water buffalos
and all the fire of Mount Merapi

we never saw him again

the night after that
if he's survived Sukarno
Suharto has surely grabbed him

the night after that
all bundled up in the woolen long johns
our whole army wears (obtainable in three sizes
                    but mostly in stock in two
                    so always too long or
                    too short
got up
in the middle of the hall
Hans   (druggist's son from Enschede
                                   RC, read Terbraak* from cover to
                                   cover, and politician without
                                   a party par excellence)
Hans called out   (he still hadn't ever
                                   said anything except that
                                   he had a brother who read a lot)
so Hans called out   (and awake right away
                                   without a tear in his eyes
                                   he stood there beside his bed
                                   Vink with his pinky on the seam
                                   of his long johns)

Hans thus called out   I swear that from now on I'll
                              never wash or shave again
                              not ever gonna clip my nails either

and I thought
sure enough
thought I
o god
Lumey* I thought
and Colijn* don't know anything
about it

"go to sleep peacefully, the government's watching over you"

ai! says Anna Marie
kisses your finger
right?
been in the madhouse twice by now
but because I'm so fancy free at needlework
that wasn't so bad
soon I'd got better
and that *madres superiores* soon saw
that I really was so good at sewing
so I showed all those other nuts how to sew
and then they'd do it like I did

it all goes to show you says Pepe of the Fonda
before and after the elections
in Spain for the First
and Second Chambers

says he:
      whoever wins
      as regards the winner
      all we oughtta be is suspicious
      whether I've voted for him
      or not

you read
in reality
the incinerating ovens were
letting out smoke
constantly
and a disgusting sweet smoke
glided in deeply between the barracks
and pervaded and permeated the place
you could literally no longer "take"
a breath
besides it was damp
and autumn

says Anna Marie
in fact just like here
years ago
the dogs had big cudgels
hanging around their neck
they couldn't attack anyone
the women too had big iron
bolts on doors and themselves
nothing could ever happen to them

but nothing is nothing to speak of
and you do have to get on with it
since going backwards doesn't make it either
indeed:
     das lagerorchester spielte lustige lieder*
didn't it
so everybody go to sleep peacefully

hardly awake that morning
10th of May 1940
the airfield at Twente bombed
hundreds of aircraft heading
westward
"so everybody go to sleep peacefully"

it was five a.m.
I was quick to be up and at 'em
down along by-ways
on my bicycle
no krauts would be coming along those paths
yet they were full
of fleeing Jews
all packed up backs sagging and been had
I reported to a reserve captain
who sighed and groaned
and said
"put on your uniform"
"here's a rifle"

"there are the cartridges"
"and your bread ration"

o you think then
cartridges a rifle
and I've never shot yet
except blanks at rabbits
but nevertheless thought I
now for sure right into the sewer
flip up the cover
and it's a manhole
but no
there was an icy silence
I didn't know anyone but André
from the highschool orchestra
he'd played first
I second violin under Kolhy*
there was
(one must say fortunately)
one old war-horse
from the KNIL (Royal Dutch East Indies Army)
(now all you've got
left over from that are a few Moluccans)
he was on leave
and screamed
"goddammit where's the gin"
the reserve captain jumped up in panic
from his chair his eyes full of fear
(thinking probably oh jeeze they're

already here)
"where's the gin? you've got to get them all
liquored up and then up and at 'em goddammit
or else they're not gonna fight
no dogface wants to die and this recipe's battle-tested
believe me I'm a pro and ate nails in hell
I do know what it takes
these birds here don't know about nothin'
but you shouldda seen them brown bastards go
one by one they dropped
to our hurrah hurrah
for Queen and Country"

> *the little Zapata asked*
> *father why are you crying*
> *because Emilio they are*
> *dispossessing us of our land*
> *why are we not fighting*
> *against them*
> *because they have the power*
> *when I am big father*
> *I will take back all our land*
> *father Zapata lay his hand*
> *upon his son's head*
> *and said (it was in 1887)*
> *good, when you are big*
> *so wipe off your tears*
> *said Zapata and have patience*

meanwhile we
(the telephone rang)
jumped up
rifle rusted up
and mood true enough
so many degrees below zero
yet we did jump up
we were thinking this is it: orders
but no said the captain flatly
that we had surrendered
by telephone
that the Germans were now across the Ijssel

> *and you think*
> *goddam*
> *a total collapse*
> *into your own*
> *bones*

and I was thinking
how do I get away from here
so I said
captain I'm gonna clear outta here
he jumped up
as if bit by a viper
and cried out:

> that's desertion
> that's the death penalty
> so I'll shoot you dead

said Anna Marie
it's clear
he smells death
ya see
just like a human
like me
so I cry out
Kissinger
o kiss me
kissinger my baby
kiss me
a baby

meanwhile I am thinking
that man is overwrought
(his wife and kids were living in Deventer
the firing line, he thought, for all he knew)
and as he said
my wife and kids are living in Deventer
so don't pull any silly stunts
I showed him my soldier's manual
article number such-and-such
a prisoner of war has the
right to escape
by international regulations
you had us surrender by telephone
so we're leaving
he didn't say much

(thinking about Deventer)
we all cut out on him

said my father later on
they conduct themselves so meticulously
they pay for everything and you don't hear about any
robberies anymore like you'd once read in history
they've even already got the money for England
on them

no it's all turned out to be quite
something else and not at all
like we learned about it in my time

said my friend Frits:

           now you're gonna see it
           the crap floating to the surface
           whereat the odor of shit
           gets sold as eau de Cologne

wrote Wieslav Kielar
in Der Spiegel:

           it's Sunday
           our camp borders
           (in Auschwitz)
           on the women's camp
           the orchestra is playing
           we go over to the barbed wire
           many people on the move

(no corpse removals
on Sunday)
I search with my eyes
(they're still there
it's a miracle too)
I look for Halina
since I have a
"rendez vous" with
Halina and on the
"main street"
(on Sunday)
it's busy like on
the street of a capital
as I said
the orchestra playing
I look for Halina
and yes there she is
tall slender among
all those women tall
and slender with blonde hair
waving in the wind
I think she sees me
I can see her hair
very light blonde
in the wind and I think
she saw me too
seen as a kind of gestural language
at least that's how I see it
and yes, it's certain

that was it she probably
wanted to thank me for
the cigarettes that I
gave by way of Edek Galinski
certainly
gestures
anyway movements
with the hand
that was the whole conversation
it was at least
a beautiful sight

says Anna Marie later:

        I got so radioactive that
        they had to lock me in
        iron chains with jesus
        above my head

        like I recapitulating
        already told you as a matter of fact
        stabbed more than three times
        in my breasts
        and that's why you see I don't wear
        (due to that radioactivity we've
        got here)
        those blue beads anymore either

a little after that

laughing:

> look we are kids
> and talking about the rules of the game
> of love we're just playing shuffleboard
> carelessly and throwing stones
> whoops once again a hole in someone's head
> and you bust your brains
> and often
> in brief
> eine Umwelt (surroundings)
> von Schwarzwälder (the Black Forest)
> in the end you know that alley
> where the cat catches the rebound
> I catch it and resound

said Pepe

we were talking about

(what were we talking about)

since Pepe just says something

he speaks for himself

not with somebody

so he said

(out of the blue)

> man is fantastic
> but you shouldn't
> see him as a whole

Catastrophy Ulli comes in

and cries out I know one

you ask
so which one
listen says Catastrophy Ulli
    a man arrives
    at the horsemarket
    in Oldenburg
    sees a magnificent horse
    black slender sound and silky
    thus superb
    and says
    it must be expensive
    the seller says
    it's real reasonable
    so how much does it go for
    500 marks
    then something's wrong with it
    such a fine horse for 500 marks
    no there's nothing wrong with it
    then why so cheap
    it was the pastor's horse
    so what. . .
    that is, it doesn't understand
    anybody saying "whoa"
    or "giddy-up"
    no stops and no goes
    oh says the man
    so what did it respond to
    the pastor did ride it
    sure

when you say O my dear lord
it goes forward
say jesus maria
and he stops
says the man
I'll buy the horse
and goes off for a ride
a magnificent horse
at a trot gallop
all so magnificent
until they arrive at the seaside
on a crag
the buyer cries out
(frightened)
jesus maria
the horse rears up
and stops
the man sighs
my dear lord

says Catastrophy Ulli
apologetically: *Ein Witz* (a joke)

as Anna Marie said earlier:
> you do have to get on with it
> since going backwards doesn't make it either
> maybe we die too soon
> we become gate-keepers
> (*die Wacht am Rhine*)

and the Shah of Persia
            is our guarantee
like he is for
            the entire West
sometimes I think I'm suspended
            on two hooks
the secondary school
            and the hospital
since you're not given anything
    you've got to inherit everything
        we've got to think more
            about uncoupling
            don't we

but
o god
whoever forgets
one hand
the other

as Cortazar has said: with her the mystery only begins
            with the explanation

says Catastrophy Ulli:
            a dreadful dream
            I sweat like a pig
            I don't think it had anything
            to do with
            that accident

or four years in the clink
standing there
at the end of my bed
and more often than this once
a black man
that is: not so much a Negro
but someone completely black
without a recognizable face
and I jump up
and walk outside
go back inside again
pour cold water over
my head and roll a joint
go back to sleep again and
wake up again really furious
and I see him standing there
but now a man that I know
who I've got nothing against
and I'm furious and want to
fight and do fight but
he does seem to be made of
rubber however I punch or
whatever I do he falls down
stands up and keeps on laughing
too. . .
now what would that be?

ah well said Uncle Jake
it's the same everywhere

what I read which is that everywhere
farming is failing for the same reason
because we're producing too much
whether that be butter or wheat
and yet it's still strange
that I've always got to read
that there's still so much
hunger in the world. . .
maybe it's all
not so well distributed

and on top of that said he:
                    it's really odd that
                    never yet has a politician ever
                    apologized for the fact that
                    ten years ago he'd made
                    a mistake we've been stuck with
                    for years or for ages

says Pepe:
        I've got another card from Bernie
        Bernie Bishop
        tu amigo
        the one who lived in your house
        that first winter
        a picture postcard with
        a piscina even bigger than that
        last one but that last one is
        already there and I don't have

room for a larger one either
so I think
I'll send that card back to him
with a letter you will write
for me in English

I write the letter
and think of Perry Street
and also of La Mama the theatre
downtown on Second Avenue
where I stood in line for tickets
and in that line were standing six
people I knew from the Fonda Pepe
and I tell him that
and he laughs
and shows me the big book
in which the names are booked of all
who've ever had a room at his place
as well as those who dropped by
made their drawings for him
which are now hanging on the walls
and he finds it all quite natural

sings Annette from Düsseldorf:

> "*Ein Freund ein guter Freund*
> *das ist das schönschte was es*
> *gibt auf der Welt*
> *Ein Freund ein guter Freund*

und so weiter. . ."
(The Comedian Harmonists)*

say I
to someone
we're walking out the door
of the house on Perry Street
West Greenwich Village
around the corner by the Sassarack
Bernie's bar
and we hear someone calling out
"Hey come over here and have some champain"
and sure enough
in the street
long tables laden with champagne
"we won the rent strike"
meaning: gained from the rentlord
new doors new windows with their frames
there's still some justice
we get into some champagne
and then on over to Sheridan Place
someone calls out
it's Melody
Melody from Formentera days
Melody who was a guest
Melody girlfriend of Big Tits Renée
the one with the boa constrictor
she calls out
I've got a book for you

but I don't have it with me
and I don't remember the title either
but something like healthful living
with lots of thoughts well-put
but I also
saw Tientje
Tientje Louw
(I thought so, I knew it and didn't know why)
(even tho she *was* living in Venice)
(even so. . .)
Tientje called to Melody who wanted
Simon Vinkenoog's* address
she's staying at the Chelsea Hotel
okay you'll get the book tomorrow
I say okay we'll go to the Chealsea Hotel
didn't see her anymore
never did see the book
did buy some picture postcards tho
on a University Street corner
Thea is walking around with the cards
she picked out the man behind the counter
it's Saturday so the Sabbath for me
and I only sell things to nice people
since actually because of my religion I'm
not open and how should I know but would you
like a shot of whiskey
I say yes
(having already seen the bottle under the counter)
so a shot of whiskey

but you've been holding on to my cards much
too long and I do want to be paid
so we pay

and I think back to sabbath
in Enschede
in 1940
in love with Jolly
Jolly Kanterman
her grandfather a rabbi
and also
secret bicycle rides
and you heard of it as if
as if the trees
or it could have been wind
probably a stench
passed it on
"he's smoochin' with a Jewess"
and also how it ended up
like she wrote later on
on that photo we had taken
because I'd wanted to go to England
"it's better to have loved
and lost
than never to have loved at all"
since it's language which fixes the relations
in the process of speaking and writing
reveals the involvement

so we go on to the Chelsea Hotel
but first go into a department store
there I see two women
one of them so beautiful
like Fritzi once said
about her mother
as beautiful as the moon on a summer's night
I say that out loud
she replies in pure Surinamese tones
Ah believe we speak the same language
we did buy that dress

I'm thinking Jolly had an elder sister
a gorgeous mother and on Fridays
when the evening star would come out
I'd put the lights out and we'd get
the tastiest bonbons and would sing Zus'
(Jolly's sister's) self-composed
French chansons
later Zus went into
public relations
(after the war)
at Menco Textiles
until there weren't any textiles anymore
and Hongkong sold where it wanted to

meanwhile we walked over to the Chelsea Hotel
there I ask for Tientje
but she had got re-married

and I didn't know who to
so I said to the man at the desk
who I knew from before
a beautiful tall blonde woman
says he, Dutch?
yes
well, room 84
you can phone her
I do that
I hear on the other end
"hello this is Albert Vogel"
I say
that's nice
he says
nice that you call
I don't say that I want Tientje
he says
I'll come downstairs
I say
I'll wait for you in the Don Quichotte
a café annex

    we do that and I can still
    see us sitting there
    Margreetje* and I
    and Machteld* and Karel*
    and Oscar* and Jan Kramer*
    and the mother of his kids
    who he legitimized by getting
    married and Karel and I were

witnesses the next day and
with Jan meanwhile writing
wildly via a wild secretary
while thinking of Jane Mansfield
who lost her head riding on
back of a motorcycle
passing a truck
that lost a
section of
steel plate

Albert Vogel comes downstairs
with a beautiful tall blonde woman
who is not Tientje
and I ask him if he's seen Tientje
says he no
she left yesterday
(I think Melody was really
more taken up with the echo
than with the song)
Vogel says
I don't have much time
I've got to go and visit
a painter
ask I: far away
yes on Christopher Street
oh, number 110
says he yes
say I: Jan Hendriksen

says he yes
but not where he lives but on
Prince Street where all the galleries
are now says he
are you coming along
say we yes
and we see Jan and we walk
up and down stairs and through
all the warehouses now empty since
ships aren't entering New York harbor
anymore a single street of art
and you've seen everything

> *fleetingly the next*
> *morning it had to be*
> *through that little window*
> *in Perry Street I saw the Maasdam*
> *as well as the Isle de France*
> *on their last voyage to New York*

says Manolo this morning
it's the thirteenth of March
(once in the Foreign Legion;
what were you supposed to do at 17
after the Civil War in Spain)
says he today which is the thirteenth
with full moon we're not going to work
the roof might even cave in
sure enough I see

falling beneath the full
moon on the thirteenth a
star with a long tail
fortunately not
on my house

he
Manolo didn't come
Anna Marie did go
she'd already said it:

> underneath this island
> lies a bomb and I have
> got to keep guard that's
> why I empty out my bags
> you see, so that later on
> I'll be getting back into
> the madhouse without
> baggage

first a little more cheerful
music and put up a few little walls
for the enclosure
and against the radiation
the ruination and the
erosion and then up and at 'em

don't forget that in Mallorca
in Palma they've got only three
mothers superior for more than

a hundred nuts so when I come
they'll be glad I can sew like the
best of 'em and I'll be appointed
the fourth mother superior for sure
so they are glad
and so am I
we speak about the rules of the
game of love we play shuffleboard
there's mass in the mornings
there's television in the evenings
we throw stones and
whoops once more a hole in
his head
I do take it into
my head
and a lot
and they're going to say
you came back stronger
than you went away weak
meanwhile you can hear
them weaving there
(and not only there)
like mad to make
a basket big enough
to hold them
all

said Terts:
        "Songs fairy tales and the important

domestic events were spun into a
strand and gradually formed a ball of
yarn. That's how a book would come
into being. Knotted writing.

add to that:
"There you have it - the thread of
the spinning wheel that spins the
yarn of Fate and at once, in the
process - the canvas of literature"

I'm walking with Bernie
under the Brooklyn Bridge
he stops
and says
do you see that threshold
I say yes
says he
that was the threshold of our house
I used to play on that
here you can see some other thresholds
but we had to clear out of here
because the bridge was being built

I walk outside
on 13 March 1979
I see an eclipse of the moon
all of us on the earth are standing
here in the form of the earth itself

between the rising full moon and the
already setting sun and we all together
cannot diminish the light of the moon
but it's still only twenty past ten

ai!
says José
they are
(he means the stars
and all the heavenly bodies
since they go on being bodies)
so thoroughly governed by instinct
that they never get around to any
knowledge

Eulalia very slowly reads:
>*Wind*
>
>*why, wind, do you make*
>*the bird's feathers ruffle*
>*watch out that you don't chill her*
>*the little chick is very frail*

and later on
after you'd been thinking about communication
and Jan Hendriksen with his 13 TVs
along the wall all thirteen of 'em on
calling out:
>the pinnacle of information
>you don't hear or see anything anymore

Thea returns from her teaching
and says Eulalia has read the last
verse of "The Wind" and
said tell it to Bert:

>Wind
>
>why, wind, do you ruffle
>the pages of my book
>watch out I want to write
>and don't be naughty

someone wrote me
now that you're going to New York you might notice a
little white house, it might be the smallest one in town
that's where my son probably lives and if you see him
tell him he's got to call up or write to his mother
tell him that
so in New York I stand before the smallest white house on
St. James Street and see a man come out of it at an age
that he stands there pissing in his little garden and
tell him he's got to write his mother a letter
she said
quickly buttons up his fly and dashes back inside

someone calls out:

>when guilt comes
>and sleep
>comes guilt

as Ismael says:

> the one on the left
>
> didn't know what the right
>
> was doing

but through the
night a scream
like never before:

> *o I miss you*
>
> *you're burning in my skin*
>
> *in my throat*
>
> *every time I breathe in*
>
> *it's as tho the void*
>
> *were rushing into my chest*
>
> *where you are not anymore*

Bernie and I do not keep on
standing upon the threshold
says he
that's not possible here
there's constant construction
and demolition going on here
even if New York were one big threshold
and it is
we'd be stepping across it
and through it

> the rich shut their trap
>
> which the poor flap open
>
> (too late)
>
> (too bad)

```
says Henry
to Bernie:     What're you doin' nowadays
says Bernie:   I'm on pension
Henry
(surprised):   on pension?
               but you're still younger than I
               (at least at school you were)
says Bernie:   I'm on pension
says Bernie
to me:         he can't stand that
               he's got to work and I don't
               do any more than I want to
says Henry:    so you're on pension
               so you've got a lot of time
says Bernie:   yeah
says Henry:    then I got a little job for ya
               every day a truckload of caviar
               okay?
says Bernie:   okay
calls Henry:   how's it going with your daughter
thinks Bernie: (o I
               I miss
               and my throat's
               on fire
               missing and empty
               that spot
               and I
               lonesome
```

            me

            and miss)
says Bernie: o man she's fine
                bigger than me
                she's got everything
                and still only sixteen
                I see her every Sunday
                you know
says Henry: so I'll see ya tomorrow

I think
that is: I remember
that the teacher said:

                        you are all
                        wood on wood
                        but know that
                        one on top of another
                        makes better burning
                        than one alone

and you dream
away and with no
thought at all you think
we were really always
more like a balloon
you'd rise
the wind would carry you along
and when it was all over
you'd land in an unknown country

that you'd already seen from above
and seemed familiar to you
only later on after you'd landed
the people were speaking
a different language

so you land in Tel Aviv
75km further on you arrive in
Mishkenot Sha'ananim
"peaceful residence"
the first house
a row of houses
built outside the walls
of the old city
of Jerusalem
by a millionaire
who wanted to do good for the people
who didn't have a house inside the walls
but outside the walls it was so
unsafe that the inhabitants did
go back into the city at night
via the David's Gate through which we
also enter the city
he also built a mill
to grind meal and bakeries
to help the people with food and
work but during the June war
the peaceful residence got seriously damaged
and now it is the property of the City of Jerusalem

a little while later you're walking

through the garden of Gethsemane

along past the house of John Ferno*

(Next Time in Jerusalem)

so into the garden and past the Golden Gate

which is closed and then descending

along the tomb of Absalom

and a little Arab boy who is guiding us

and hugs Thea suddenly says

now kneel for a moment and we do that

and he asks

when he has stood up again

and so do we and he sees that

and believes that we believe what

he has seen and believes

he says

now stand up and we will go further

we stood up and went further

I saw in the trees the hair

which Absalom clung to

and we heard nothing but that

silence which descended slowly from

Gethsemane to that spot

Eulalia reads

(after so many lessons

already far past the pipe

that papa was smoking)

she reads:

listen to the woods
how they are rustling
the trees
it's the wind
blowing through the branches

see how the golden leaves
fall through the gusts of wind
and cover the earth

it's the autumn wind
look how the leaves
that are left on the trees
tremble with fear

hear how they talk
and scream while
the wind tugs on them
and they don't want to let go

says the little boy
a little Arab boy
so now to a school
to Turnat

for a moment the Dome of the Rock
stood as still as a lightning bolt

and behind the dark walls the whole
city was on fire

so Turnat
says the little boy
a school for cooks say we
(showing him a photograph)
he nods vaguely
Turnat says he then very sure
is where we go now and there
is also a school there
we never arrived at the baker's school
tho we did come to a school
wanted to give him some money
did so
and upset insulted furious
he dashed it onto the ground

Sadat sits with Begin
in the King David Hotel
they're no longer sitting there
but they keep on having sessions
"all over the place"
and Carter is paying for his
reelection with them

said Mr. Brunn
Lisa's father
Lisa who always brought an incredibly little

doggie along with her to the Fonda
don't believe any of that
after so many years of war
peace only comes slowly
meanwhile people were dancing in the streets
of Jerusalem and thought finally it's over
and we'll become just a state among states
said the taxi driver who brought us
to the museum
look what Begin offered wasn't much at all
what were we supposed to do with all that land
we started out small
that was enough
peace
yeah a peace that the flock
grazes for

his bodyguard said
look when those Arabs came
we normally had to shoot them

but in the café it just went on like it did
like with Eulalia's lesson
in which it said that two dogs
did not fight over one bone
no, over two piles of bones
which lay on the left and the right
sides of the street
the two dogs however were tied together

by a rope so short that neither of them
could get at the bones if he at all
wanted to have his own pile on the right or left
the rope offered no opportunity for that
so this is how
(due to their hunger or insight or both)
came to the conclusion to first together
eat up the bones piled at the left and then the right
whereby they thus both got what they wanted

you sit watching soccer on TV
the commentator calls out :

                                          there was no equalizer

and said they
also those who
were forgotten
you do know we come from
that night and mist
and still buy light
that costs more and more
and gives out less and less light

and it could've been
so lucid
as Margreetje's mother
said it so well:

                    as it was put by Spinoza
                    Reason pure the purest of
                    Reason set down responsibly

and passed on as a model
of harmony which without dash or
flash will remain unrecognizable
for good and all and without being
seen as Spinoza put it ground down
into the finest lens of vision
says Eulalia
(later at the seaside)
while looking for scallops
(that looked like Chinese hats)
which you've got to pluck from the rocks
with a knife
says Eulalia
(as she stops)
well where is Holland
you look to the north
or north-west actually
and you say
there!
but why do you want to know that
because then I
when I'm here by myself
looking for scallops
can stop and look
in that direction
and then know where you live
and we'll always know about each other

said Tut:

if you dream about someone
they say you're thinking
about that someone
I dream a lot
about my mother
who also used to hit me
a lot
and of Mr. Frans
Uncle Frans who gave me a
flying dutchman pedal-car from my father
who never saw me but
was born a Behmstein
so my name is also
Behmstein
my mother sung
wasn't Jewish
so I'm actually
porky and Jewish
half then but with
a lot of pork

Indeed
the whole earth is floating
in a tremendous sea
with all of us
upon it or under it

says she:

     I was in Lourdes

     since I do love saints

I asked:

     surely you went to visit

     the Curative Cave every day

says she:

     no

     I'm not even sick

     I took a cable car all the way up

     to the top

     of the Pyranees and saw

     all of Spain and France in

     one smashing glance

man at times

mouth open and invisible

tucked up in a coat just enough

for the rain insufficient

for the wind

         next a slope to cope with

         snow-white the way up

said Mr. Brunn

in Jerusalem

(Lisa's father)

Lisa told us about you

from Formentera

says he:

> don't believe in peace with Arabs
> who from the start only wanted
> to drive us into the sea
> if that peace ever comes
> it will take years

as Lisa assured us go to my parents we got there and her
mother is française and Brunn her father from Hungary
and when we got there an uncle was sitting there who
wanted to look at soccer came there to eat every day
and couldn't understand that the soccer game was called
off or to fill in for it a round of chess
says Mr. Brunn
we met
my wife and I
in Beirut the most
beautiful city in the world
completely cosmopolitan
my wife was in the French liberation corps
and I in the Haganah
we were married there in Beirut
but watch out for
peace too soon
since:

> with ten bricks
> you don't make anything
> with a hundred something
> with a thousand a little house

if you don't fling those thousand
at each other's head

I hear Tut say:
        it might well be
        that out of a deep sleep
        it was suddenly told to us
        and we would know exactly
        about the question and answer
        I was in Fatima in Portugal
        and there then they did know it
        even tho it was a long trip

you see
before you know it
you're involved in a furious fugue
onward onward
there's never an end to
le point d'orgue (fermata)

next Tut said
"inspired":
        they took a picture
        me sitting way up there
        in the cable car
        with so much outlook
        far above any curing
        but I had to have him do it over
        I looked bad on it

and if you're already not pretty
that's not acceptable
besides that I'm not sick
also wrote the snackbarman
around the corner a card
gives me coffee every day
and a piece of mocha cake
so I write him
and also when I became fifty
he gave me fifty guilders
and I thought about Uncle Frans
who when I was a child
when no-one thought about me
gave me a flying dutchman pedal-car
even tho I was born in Berlin
born a
Behmstein
said Bernie:
after a few shots of whiskey
it could be possible of course
that at the peak of a deep sleep
you can get an exact answer to
questions you weren't even able
to ask yourself
so the questions and answers correspond
just like I wrote in
"Daddy's Day" the only story
I ever wrote
say I:

that could be

Eulalia reads again about the wind
that has to be careful with the leaves
on the trees especially when they are still young
they *could* fall off

thinking about learning to read and write now she also
thinks about first learning to ride a bicycle when
she was thirty in San Miguel on Ibiza and suddenly as
she says the distances get shorter than walking that you
saw more too but then again less because you rode past
plenty which however was not bad because you had always
while walking already seen all there was and where you
now came to fresh on the bicycle was not quite the same
since you had never really in walking been there

and on the day (March the 22nd)
when the ambassador from England
got shot in his car in the Hague
and his manservant too
calling in a loud voice is
Paco Luna
who's drilling us a well
calls he:
      agua!
      water!
      y buena
      and good

y dulce
and sweet
at 16 meters deep

we also get a short letter from Anna Marie
in Mallorca:

> fortunately I'm back in the madhouse again
> I'm teaching them all sewing and knitting and
> I think I'll surely get promoted too but not
> like you might think right away up to deadly
> blessedness where Mario must now be with so
> many others also that I do at times think
> there's some calling coming from the depths
> of that vast space and I believe I recognize
> that voice which of course I can't ever forget
> that's why I'm here altho I know that nothing
> and no-one comes back in the same form as the
> one in which he or she presented themself
> when they were still among us. . . ave vale
> amen. . .

but for Breton sinning and being born were
not the same thing, as Octavio Paz has observed and also
this next text:

> via the word we can regain
> the lost kingdom. . .
>
> language is not the symbol of the Fall
> of Man but of our original innocence

the word has its roots in a
silence which precedes
speaking precedes speech
a presentiment of language
then comes the silence after the word
and between these two silences
moves the poem

I ask Bernie:

do you have a woman now
(he's had plenty and
pretty ones but never for so
long)
says Bernie:
(without having to
think about it):

they come they go
but they all talk too much

a girl from Switzerland tells us:

look my parents live in
a village in the mountains now
for twenty years and when they
arrived there they'd come from
very far away because going
from one valley to the other
is always over the mountain and
thus different and it took a very long

125

time before the neighbors would greet
the strangers and now after twenty years
they've got to greet all the people in
that upward coiling ribbon village
and are getting home later
and later. . .

indeed
vulnerability needn't
be proved
it's an established fact
because everyone who
is different
is no good

we invite Bernie out with a girlfriend
of ours who constantly talks and dine
together in Chinatown
she talks constantly
Bernie listens
she goes on talking in the Sassarack
and now after that they've been talking
for years always together

you think:

> *there's a point*
> *in which everything comes together*
> *and after that*
> *everything goes together*
> *the other way*

so we go to Mexico

Eulalia reads:

> *snail snail*
> *let's see your horns*
> *come out of the cabbage*
>
> *don't you hide*
> *in your little house*
> *today you must*
> *go running with*
> *another snail*
> *which my little pal*
> *caught today*
>
> *snail snail*
> *stick your horns*
> *into the sun which*
> *your daddy has*
> *also done*

imagine, said Einstein, two people traveling in two
spaceships at different speeds and that both spaceships
had a gigantic clock that the travelers could look at
from spaceship to spaceship as well as their own. Each
traveler would think that his clock was running its
normal way but that the one on the other was slow. If one
of the spaceships was moving faster than the speed of light
the traveler in the other spaceship would think the first

one's clock had stopped. In popular terms: when checking
your wristwatch you suppose it's always running just as
fast. Wrong: you think that because you're always looking
at your watch from the same place. . .

maybe
thinks Bernie
that vacant threshold
beneath the Brooklyn Bridge
got taken at last
(or do I think that)

but how does it go
you have a friend who is married to a girl-friend of ours
from Formentera where she was then still living with
Achmed who made beautiful birds out of driftwood and lost
feathers and came from Egypt
she didn't know Jorge yet who she later met in Mexico City
when she was on vacation there and who played violin
I didn't know Andrea
Thea did know her and both lose sight of
each other

> *what one eye loses*
> *the other one*
> *however does*
> *find again*

Thea got a letter from London in which Andrea wrote that
she had met Swedish Jan who had her address and that she
would come to visit us which she did with her husband Jorge

they said: if you ever come to Mexico you can
              stay with us
we say: we'd love to
we meet Homero Aridjes, Mexican poet
in Rotterdam at Poetry International and asks
would you really like to go to Mexico
to give a few readings at universities
I say yes
then we'll arrange that
we meet a week before we're to go
Tonny Zwollo a female architect who wants to get her
doctorate under Aldo* with a thesis in which she makes
clear that she wants to build like a child that conquers
and gives shape to space crawling on all fours
a constructive game
she asks if we will take along a package
for Martin Ruiz her boyfriend in Mexico
we say yes
we do that
we arrive in Mexico City
and hear that Andrea has
died a few days earlier
of breast cancer which she
as Jorge said already had when
she was staying with us and we knew
nothing about it and she hadn't wanted to
be operated upon because it was already too far gone

she'd said
said Jorge
that she
from the knife
didn't expect
anything anymore

and here
said he
is the key
to our house
that's how she wanted
it and me too

he also said
she went on working
till the last mom-
ent a snail

in her shell
in and out
till the end

he showed it to us
paintings drawings
beaches shells and often
also from the beach back into
the distance still that solitary boat
back after all in the catch

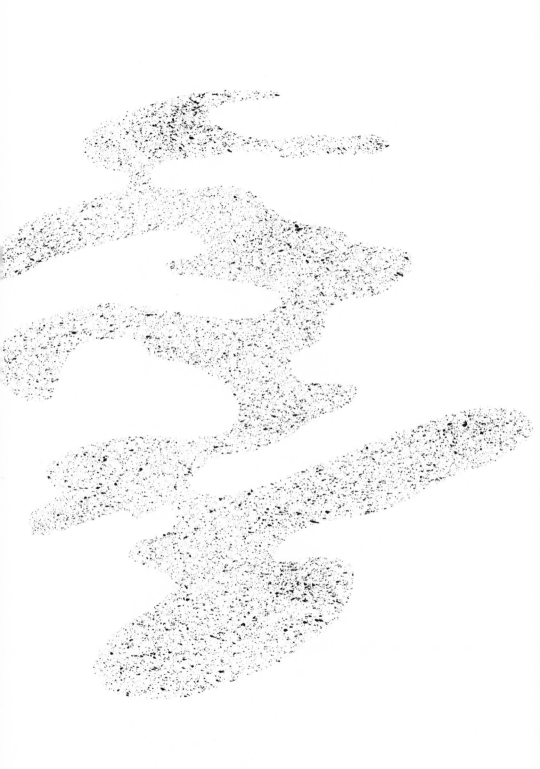

of an outlook turned inward
into the shell of a sea snail
full of mother-of-pearl and song

and you hear it
and you think
the world is full
completely full/
empty
very slowly Eulalia reads
and also writes it down

> *birds*
> *what are you asking me*
> *tell me*
>
> *why do birds fly?*
> *to amuse you*
> *since they know*
> *that you are here*
> *and looking into the sky*
>
> *and how do they know that*
> *because they can see from*
> *far away that you have*
> *the face of an*
> *angel and want*
> *to fly off*
> *with them* we bring the presents of Tonny Zwollo to Martin Ruiz'

office of the the Patrimonio Nacional de los Arqitectos
on the Insurgentes and he says thank you and would you
like to borrow my car for four weeks since I'm going
to Europe we say yes, we'd love to
we get a Ford Maverick and drive away arrive in
Chitzen Itza Thea climbs up a temple loses her nerve
to climb down asks two kids a blond one and a dark-
haired one a Mexican will you show me the way down
the stairs in Spanish the kids say *si* she calls down to
me in Dutch that if these kids hadn't helped her she'd
still be up on that Temple the blond kid says in Dutch
o do you come from Holland weeks later we get a letter
from my father in which he writes you two have met a
son of a friend of mine we realize that we had seen
that friend at Frank Martinus Arion's* farewell party
he went on to say my son is in Mexico and is studying
guitar a year later we get the news that he's married
to a Mexican girl and that we are invited but the news
reaches us in Jerusalem where Geula Dagan is just telling
us that if you're looking for someone whose first name
is Lisa that's no problem there are very few Lisas and
her parents are named Brunn and they live here around
the corner she tells us as we're about to leave and have
seen her paintings from the door of her house overlooking
the old wall and David's Tower about the little boy who
was always playing with his balls about which his parents
were *very* concerned and so sent him to a
psychiatrist who asked him why he did that and that
that distressed his father and mother and that

naturally he had those balls but didn't he have other
toys at hand. . .
at which the little boy said that he was always *very*
lonely since his parents even worked in the evening when
that wasn't necessary but that they'd got so used to it
because of the kibbutz in which they always had to work
day and night then there *was* always the crèche for him
and not any more now that they'd gone to live in the city
and so he was often left *very* alone. . .
and that's why the psychiatrist says come back next week
and think about your parents that little boy does do that
and thinks about his parents but his parents only about
his balls and comes back and the psychiatrist says after
a telephone call that unfortunately I've got to be gone
a little while on an emergency case but I'll be back in
a jiffy the little boy sits there all alone behind the
psychiatrist's big desk and knows that he's not allowed
to play with his balls and searches for and finds something to do and discovers a big box of bonbons no doubt
a present from a patient and hesitates but not for long
opens the box and begins one by one to eat up the bonbons
. . . the psychiatrist comes and sees that and gets furious
and cursing calls out: "why didn't you play with your balls"

I come across Anna Marie
completely cheered up who
says:

      yeah I'll tell you I was completely
      confused I just dropped doing

everything and went to
Mallorca and they gave me some
good medicine and see I feel
better than ever it was
such a big mess when I got
back home of course that's
because before I left I
just dropped everything
and that gets back
at you

and then too:

                we've naturally got to look out
                now that the world gradually
                and hand over fist
                (on *one* belly)
                has become *one*
                television program

once again we're on the way from Palenque to
Cristobal de Las Casas and I hear amidst the
mist high in the mountains ten kilometers per
hour very far in the distance Jolly's voice
and we lay together underneath a tree
said she:
    now
    now I want everything
    all the way
    along came

a farmer
nothing happened
at all

by turns we call up Jorge "larga distancia" from Cristobal
de Las Casas to Mexico City expectantly sit I upon the
Plaza and have my shoes polished along comes a tall man
too big for all of Chiapas sits beside me and I'm Piet
Grotenboer from Tilburg says he and I paint we do
in the long run get Jorge and tells us there was a
package for us at his place delivered by a Dutchman
Jules who he hadn't seen but that as he lay on the beach
at La Ventosa in Tehuantepec with two girls who he'd
met at a reading I'd held at the UNAM the University
of Mexico City a man lay there of whom one of them
Adriana asked what time it was and that was this Jules
who had delivered our package. . .
later Jorge was to marry Adriana

there is always
somewhere in a wall
a sordid cricket calling
that by doing nothing
all things get done

only your own sound
can save you
since you've got to
sing anyway

137

in front of the Capitol in Washington DC sit
Sadat Begin and Carter and sign a peace treaty
that Carter pays for with others' money and
they keep on sticking plumes in each other's
hats and feathers into their asses
there was no agreement between the lines
there was no great joy in Israel
the question remained
how could it be that it
began with Begin
and the Palestinians remain the Jews
of the Arabs. . .

we arrive in Oaxaca at the same time as Lopez Portillo
who is traveling throughout Mexico with ten busloads of
supporters and occupies city after city so first in
Tehuantepec which we entered and every bed was occupied
but no problem Tonny Zwollo's friend Martin Ruiz had
said you just go to my friend in Oaxaca also an architect
and you ask him for the key to our house in El Punto a
house in the mountains we did that and came across him
just as he was leaving his office and asked him if he'd
got the letter from Martin at which he said no he hadn't
and also when he heard that we had come to get the key
embarrassed declared that he was just planning to go there
because he wanted to be there this weekend with his wife
and kids but he said suddenly relieved that means of course
that if we're there we're not here so you two can stay

in our house till we get back that we did and when they
got back and we arrived in El Punto we were passionately
greeted by the campesinos who lived in a completely see-
through house and we thought we had the key which was
not the case but luckily we could get inside through
the window

we could see at night
        they told us since
        there is electric light everywhere
        the neighbors move around inside a Chinese
        lantern their house of banana leaves
        said they in a poor country we're
        constantly confronted with
        the law of the strongest
        and the strongest are
        the others
they move around in a sea of stagnation
light within which their house is suspended
and when the TV is turned on the myth of
centuries returns to life all drugged up
up the steps of the temple where Tlaloc
awaits their warm hearts they will go
forever as it is the season of his sorrow
the light must be fed and Tlaloc awaits
lying on his back his belly a basin to
catch the blood for Tlaloc brings rain
fecundity maize and the blood of
children is the best and

most unspoiled food

and said my friend
children die
the fastest on the
battlefield as has
been proven they are
the best for that

rattling in the wind
an empty can the cat
looks for shelter
from the wind
and by the fire

in Munich Peter Jung built a
house of comforts with everything
in it and to it modern kitchen TV
the most expensive and luxurious of
the costliest the consumption society
has to offer and he's going to photograph
it and as he's snapping the photo of
what there was remains and
the rest gets blown up
this art is called: Blow-Up Art
indeed:
 there's a request for some water
 and it comes back as blood
 says Tlaloc with belly in the

sun that's how the season of sorrows
will disappear with bloodshot
ears all those children who
are no longer to intervene
since dispatched to the
place of the enigma
wandering off to all quarters
ach says Annette:

> *das Leben ist ein Hühner Leiter*
> *von lauter Scheisse kommt man*
> *nicht hinauf* *

Eulalia reads
very slowly
almost spelling:

> *If I were a balloon*
> *I'd climb very very high*
> *so that I'd be able to see*
> *from way up there the earth*
> *which is completely round*
>
> *if I could get to the*
> *top of the church tower*
> *I would stop the clock*
> *in the clocktower so*
> *that time stood still*
> *and perhaps I'd always*
> *be a child*

after that she rewrote it
and retold it with her own
words which were the same ones

didn't we?
when did we fly for the first time
in that awfully small first little car
of Zoef ("Buzz") 's to Callantsoog
buzzing past the Zwanemeer (Swan's Lake)
and then in and out of the hotel and over the
dunes and then the kiosk and then the sea and
back again and in two weeks was with Zoef,
Hols and Paula who was expecting Pietje who
was later to be named Jan and Margreetje and I
the bill for the drinks higher than the hotel's
and Buzz at that time humming away in that
Fiat mushroom and back again to yet with ever
and again right at hand a beautiful blonde who
had nothing against a single bed then too along
came Smitje of the cartographic institute to
chart the Zwanemeer and to do that had to look
deep into the glass to be able somewhat to
imagine the bottom of that lake somewhere
near sunset more or less succeeds and we
were in high spirits because what we
knew about the future was not in
our minds at all and only a fire
late at night in the dark on
a farm in the polder after

swimming naked gave us a vague
idea that things could happen which
in reckless certainty were not suspected

and so
at night
said Buzz then
such a little fiat
how had we ever
thought such a mushroom
much later
and that everything does
look like cotton
candy
and you're not
aware of
the long-term
effects of that
like that bird that
flew over Japan
and wasn't aware
of Hiroshima either
and when he found out
went off his rocker
with a lock
on his throat

o said the taxi driver
that Begin had to be

the beginning because he too
was a hawk

and we saw Sadat kneeling
deeply forward on his head
a bump from praying
and fistulas on his shoulders
and at that time he was more
in love with Hitler

it would also be nice
thinks Peter Jung
to photograph Doodewaard*
because it's named
as such

"For though thy people Israel be as the
sand of the sea, *yet* a remnant of them
shall return: the consumption decreed
shall overflow with righteousness."
ISAIAH: 10: 22

says Judith* my sister's son
was killed in that punitive expedition
against the Palestinians who had put
that bomb in that bus in Tel Aviv

question:
    where are the scales of

and what is righteousness
and my sister, she went on to say, has
been studying Arabic for more than a year

and you do come
said Octavio Paz
by good luck
or bad luck
out of the labyrinth
of solitude
you're suddenly standing outside
and ho!
you run up the stairs
again
since for god's sake no heart
with it
you cannot live
and Tlaloc laughs
the wrath of all those
dead gods
upon the living
has no end

we went swimming in the Dead Sea
full of phosphatic mud
for rheumatism and all calci-
fication and with Massada in the distance
and still further on Sodom
does make you think a moment

I turn around
I'm made of salt
and hardly of
righteousness

       o you think then
       swarm out to all
       quarters
       and you spread out
       since as had been said
       it's incredible
       history becomes predictable
       and makeable
       say the German
       thinking models

Eulalia counted to 1000 today
and José for the first time
in his life installed downstairs
a window
he had thought about that a lot
since he always thinks doubly
as in principle he doesn't want to remember anything
I haven't got any memory says he
and at that laughs relieved
since he is sly
people with too much memory says he
are never free always think backwards and forwards
at once and at the moment

that you can take the stones along for
nothing they think about something else
and I take those stones along with me

Tut went on a trip to Liège
made a visit to the Ursuline's convent
the place where she'd been to school years ago
upon arrival she asked: Parlez vou Flemish
said the sister who opened the door:
yes
she asked for the mother superior she had known
said the sister she died but we have another
one and brought Tut over to her
the mother superior and the sisters showed her
around the convent and were glad that she had
come to visit they gave her tasty things to eat
all day long when she was
leaving Tut asked: is it still so
expensive here?
what do you mean, would you like to come back
asked the mother superior
not at all I want my school fee back
since I never learned anything here

later we go on a trip with her to Nevers
since because she had been to Lourdes she's also
got to go to Nevers where Saint Bernadette
who at the time was so saintly she died of TB
lies in a small glass coffin

since Tut loves saints, the royal family and Den Uyl*
days before we left she asked if we couldn't take
with us a piece of thick plastic or canvas
in the car
I ask why
because we then if we see a cat or dog along the road
that's been hit by a car can take it with us
I say we're not going to do that
once we're underway she cries out every time
since she's got to sit in front in back she
gets queasy she says in front it's simply more
comfortable and she can see everything so
a dead cat or dog too once in a while she cries out
ooh ooh until we were fed up and we say that for every
time she does it again she's got to pay a riksdaalder
(dollar) she doesn't cry out ooh ooh ooh anymore but says
beaming I do know that I'm not allowed to say anything. . .
we talk about Berlin Savigny Platz
she becomes lyrical

> *at Savignyplatz my mother sang*
> *this fish costs more the more they*
> *get harder to catch and later on*
> *never more*
> *the sea now gets divided up in*
> *a completely different way than before*
> *when totally undivided it belonged to*
> *those who had it*
> *so my mother there sung she*
> *and it cost more than the diversion*

she presented and yet was respected
by the public
my father in boots marched in
and pulled in the trout and what
he caught he lost to my mother
my queen

we approach Nevers on the Loire
and before her skimming across the
waters a second face underneath a hat
full of feathers "Sunset Boulevard"
she cries out loud with Gloria Swanson
and thinks she "she goes on singing goddammit
after her death" but can't hit me any more

Sunset Boulevard she has seen twenty times
for sure just like "Rooie Sien"* since besides
saints the royal family and Den Uyl she loves
films the most but sex films are dirty. . .

in Nevers
Bernadette does
indeed lie emaciated and
reduced by tuberculosis
in a small glass coffin

                    so small
                    and yet so saintly
                    I wonder about that
                    thought Tut and bought

149

sometimes indeed
you think you see it
but you are blinded
by the light until
a hole falls into it

I think about Alain Teister*
(Jacques Broersma) afflicted by
the Roman Catholic faith
who died of his drinking
because he wanted to live
and had to be constantly in
temptation

> *hot breath escaped*
> *from the wall of our*
> *countenance a wound*
> *of ages and revenge*
> *on the flock*

> *it was rubbish*
> *and it kept ahead*
> *of lust and shame*
> *above the evil eye*
> *of the Trinity*
> *screwed into its joints*
> *many a crosier straightened out*

as Jacques also said:

        about acrobatic twins
        triplets and multituplets
        one can be very amazed
        clouds on the wall of our
        countenance burst
        children get eaten
        and all the forbidden meat
        no angel is safe anymore

        female bishops
        pounced on by the internal
        brute
        denied for ages

Tut
(who'd slept bad that night)
said
I was pounced on by a big bear
just then on the way to Jesus
upon the Sugar Loaf Mountain in Rio
I was nearly there
I had to go to the zoo
why?
to see how big the bear was

you think of her
in her night full of dreams
her head sad

and stewed red
unswervingly on the way
she sees the forerunners in
the rear guard of her life
a new beginning

she sighs then too:

> if only I'd been a hostage
> in that train at Wijster*
> I'd now have 3000 guilders
> smart money
> I could go to Rio

Eulalia and José come to bake bread
Eulalia kneads the dough and José stokes
the oven with fagots he'd fetched
on his back
looking when he arrived
ever so slowly
like a walking bush
very briefly I think of baker Broekema
in Beerta* and his man how they stood
there kneading and forming and carving on
the top and let it rise and then into the
oven cries out José impatiently Eulalia
the oven is now just right hurry up since he
knows that Eulalia isn't the quickest *get
moving* o goddam if it were up to you you'd
still be sitting in your mother's belly

in fact even back then bakers would scream
real loud at ovens and at the last moment
you were actually allowed to stuff your own
kneaded birdie or sheep into the hot oven

      a smiling Jimmy Carter watches
      how Begin and Sadat together
      eat up a bowl of porridge that's
      gotten starchy from his dollars. . .
      from his dollars
      his dollars
      dollars
      meanwhile thousands flee out of
      Harrisburg Pennsylvania because
      the nuclear reactors from their dollars
      their dollars
      dollars
      turn out to be not as safe as all
      the experts smilingly reassuringly
      have claimed and claim
      from their dollars
      their dollars
      dollars

Mamadubah came in on his all-wood crutch
just flown over from Liberia by the Dutch firm
for which he'd been working and among other things
drove around with the wages across the plantation and
that's why they forced him off the road to rob him where

as he said slyly smiling I didn't have anything on me
but did break my hip and then he asked:
which way is east
and he spreads his little rug between the hospital beds
and with broken hip proving later to be even more shat-
tered he bowed down and prayed toward the east persever-
ingly he prostrated himself moved by Allah's immovable
power and force of incomprehensible words
Zuster Vijgen (Nurse Figs) converses with the under-
developed regions via onomatopoeias
pork = oink oink
chicken = cluck cluck
beef = moo moo
mutton = baa baa
the Moroccans of the cleaning service do his wash
and give him a clean burnoose every day
the washing leads to some confusion
when the nurse comes and wants to wash him underneath
he starts cooing with delight and points proudly at
his erect dick
the nurse not to be embarrassed by a little incident
nevertheless does get replaced the next day by an
orderly
Mamadubah asks us:
                    don't you have this problem?

Arrad called up I've got to go to
London goddammit just when Sadat is coming
party called off

we say okay then we'll go to the sheep market
along the wall of the Old City
right near the fork in the road
to Mount Scopius and Jericho
we walk by Geula Dagan's house
she asks what are you two going to do
go to the sheep market
okay may I go with you
we meet Dropont who says
I live on a piece of land
I've got a horse goats and sheep
built my own house
I pay taxes since I spend a number
of months a year in the army
and yesterday I opened up a well
that's been there more than 10,000 years
opened up and cleaned up
no-one else has done that
but I did it
so it's my well
no I'm not going to invite you for a meshouin*
I know so many Arabs
I can't accept the invitation of one
without insulting all the others
besides I just came to see how
it's going with that Arabian gray (horse)
I see: better
so no invitation
I live with the Bible

sighs Geula:
    changing a circle
    becomes a viscious

actually
you usually didn't need to go any further
than your own house
to see what was happening across
the border
to know that there are
no borders
to what happens
you dream:
    tremendously feathered
    without feathers
    underneath trees
    without leaves
    they come in again
    across the Bering Strait
    icicles their eyes

    whizzing past goes a van
    full of music and Chinese lanterns
    buy a balloon
    a skin filled
    with nothing

    suspended in the sky like

the virgin of Guadalupe
together we catch in the act
a void
a mouth full of teeth

Confucius and Laotse meet
says Confucius later on:

      I know how the hunter
      catches the deer
      I know how the fisher
      catches the pike
      but today I saw
      the dragon
      and don't understand
      how it flies

at the market of La Junilla he sits
a voice says:

      you can leave
      he remains sitting under
      a huge sombrero
      since he is a singer
      says he
      and it is the last day
      of the year
      he remains sitting
      he is free
      tomorrow he will bring some wood
      now he is free

drinks
and gets a grip on the loss
the word

and from the labyrinth of solitude he sings
o do I have to depart
like this so alone
the way the flowers
wither and won't
anything of mine
my name or
my fame remain
here on earth
do I have to. . .
no
at least flowers
at least songs

Eulalia counts very fast from 10 to 1,000
and later on reads:
Carlos and Maria had to
laugh very hard when
they saw that man
standing on his head. . .

my friend wrote:
it's hard to tear yourself loose from
the New York drunkenness where the
madness and drunkenness are absorbed

into daily life the pressure of on and
on and on that fanaticism like there are
still those gondolas in Venice and the
red busses in London with the bowler hats
and the little glass of wine and piece of
camembert in Paris and the monkey-brain
eating Afrikaners and the snake charmers
in Tangier and the white bears of the
North Pole and the forty million
Japanese in Tokyo who eat forty
million ants per day. . . we'll soon be
back to Amsterdam. . .

Chris was standing at the seashore
alone said he and then a bastard too
when a great panic overtook me
a twilight that overwhelmed
my mind and everything
came back
my wistful youth
my father who I didn't
know and yet did visit one time
to see him and then said I've got no time
I've got to eat and all those other little chores
and failures and then too a few good things since
even tho I'm a bastard and I've had a lot of setbacks
in life I'm really not a pessimist and I can do all
kinds of things I can cook I'm a cook I can serve
people and please people I can listen and learn

and the way I'm living now I can live very happily
with my wife and little kid happier than ever
altho I've been married before and I've got
another kid but I never see that one anymore
since the man she's got now looks a lot
like me and that's good so I'm very
happy in fact and yet I think that
that's because I was standing here
at this seashore and have
found my horizon
I've prayed
I don't know
who to
but I prayed
I surrendered
to my own horizon
with that I'm now living

> *a singer*
> *alone with himself*
> *his voice fills*
> *one song*
> *with the other*

as they say:

> *the triviality*
> *of the mystery*
> *of every day*
> *birds*
> *while flying*

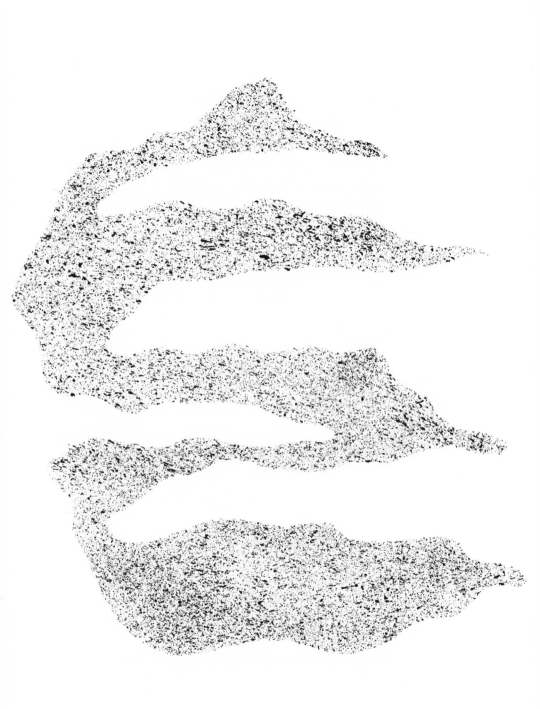

leave behind

their flight

a dancer dances

an empty space full

and if he dances on

he dances it

empty again

nostalgia grows

beyond the limits

says Uncle Jake:

ah well that's just how things are

real life as seen from a village

is always somewhere

else

but as seen from the village

it also sees through

into the city

and it isn't anywhere else

so ever and again back

to the spot

(with the words)

the spot is the encounter

(of the words)

by word

said Grandma near the end:

go to our grandparents

in Finsterwolde there they

lie buried and tell them

it's getting very quiet here

163

                         they say nothing
                         nothing any more
and Grandpa
he had never smoked
never drank never swore
and was my father's father
and just when he turned 80
on his birthday a house full of people
cigars and drinks were being handed around
and he suddenly stands up
bangs his fist upon the table
and calls out: goddammit I also want
                         a cigar and a drink
                         goddammit I want everything
when the first shock was over
he did from then on get everything and
every day until he died
he never swore any more

ah well
traveling said the man
we don't need to anymore
the world is completely familiar
because of the picture postcards
and the photographs that we
take of them

just watch out his brother cried out
before you know it it will all be the same

and you'll also lose all the other things
said Juana from Chile
in Rome things are all different
we were living in Trastevere
we didn't have a cent and I had no raincoat
in Trastevere nobody had anything and what they
didn't have they stole
the ringleader of the car thieves came over to me
with a leather jacket that I refused it was very
beautiful but I was afraid of one day coming
across the owner
okay he said: wait a week I'll bring
you one from a tourist
that's how we'd get everything there
there's also a café there
which is frequented only by priests and bishops
the priests serve the bishops
I was sitting there very quietly
and they served me too
in Trastevere we all lived together
the doctor the priest the thieves
everybody knew everything about everybody
poverty kept you together
you did have to live
how it didn't matter
like the big time operators steal on a large scale
we'd steal on a small scale
but never within the community

we were on the way
with an apple pie
to visit Francesca and her husband
a farewell visit
we were going to leave Mexico City
for home
so on to Francesca's and her husband's
house
their home is a lean-to between
two real houses
partitioned off by some boards
in that house live Francesca and her husband
seven children and a niece from Guadalajara
we arrived and got cognac and saw
how in the small space a sort of entresol
was suspended
it hung there
and upon it were hanging
two gleaming new bicycles
bicycles never used to ride on
they just hung there
like Sèvres vases standing in the homes
of the rich
said Francesca's husband
it's now going good for us
it's better to live between two
houses like we do now
we came from Chiapas and didn't have anything
now we live between two houses

that's better
when we got there we laid a blanket
on the ground with four stones one
on each corner and we crawled under
that and that's how we became citizens
in this city and we built a house of boards
and tin cans and from this tin plate we made
a little stove and upon this stove we started
to bake tacos which we sold and we bought
more cornmeal for more tacos and sometimes
some greens and later even chicken and
then we had stuffed tacos to sell
first very cheap but as we put more
into them always at a little higher price
and that's how we met one of the owners
of one of the houses we now live in between and he
asked us to come and live in between these houses
and to help him at his service station then we had
a home for nothing but that didn't last long since
I then went to ask for wages for myself and my
two oldest sons he said okay but then right away
that's the rent for the house

one more time
Zapata's dream

> *his father*
> *lays his hand*
> *upon his head*

father why are you crying

> *they are stronger*
> *look at the flowers*
> *how they blossom*

father why don't we
take back what they
took away from us

> *they are stronger*

father I'm getting
stronger and I'll
take and give everyone
back everything

> *father says nothing*

Zapata
did it
and got murdered

walking was she
Tut like a cat
in the damp grass
just before we were to see
Bernadette in the little glass coffin
and said
after she had taken in everything
well for herself the little house
in which we were pleased to stay
rest assured
I'll never need to come back here

then she crossed the road
as perfect as an incomplete sentence
her feet went
their way
below an overlong overcoat
and she said decidedly
I'm not from the country
I'm from the city

for a moment I thought about Aunt Annie
who spoke about pure reason
and then in the true sense of the word
that is she said: liking the true word
the word that is true to sense
the true sense in a true word

> *you see them crossing over*
> *so many of them crossing over*
> *the living and the dead crossing*
> *together and while crossing as*
> *well as greeting they extend*
> *and reduce the immense distance*
> *which is and is not there*

says José look if my brother and my mother
(after an also for him incomprehensible quarrel)
want to come back the door will be open a moment
like when they left
the same door

Eulalia reads:

> *The sea*
> *The sea is blue magnificent immense*
> *All of the sea is salt water*
> *The sea's waters move and make waves*
> *The sea in the distance seems a straight*
> *line*
> *That's the horizon*
> *On the sea sail ships*

says Pepe
now when we've caught a very big fish
you two have to come to eat says Pepe
and Catalina says when he's caught that
big fish says Pepe you two come to eat
but now Pepe says the wind is blowing
much too hard to catch such a big fish
but as soon as it's caught you come to
eat with us. . .

Pepe added to that:

> years ago yes
> but we've got more and more of now
> and less and less of then
> on top of that we're not going
> on a trip to Argentina
> as long as I can go on fishing here
> what for

170

you've got to know how to arrange
your life
as pleasantly as possible
he hasn't got a need to fly
nor Catalina to cross the sea

indeed
as Beerling* said:
the concept is something
that doesn't tremble
or cheer
my friend wrote
you remember Jumbo that guy
from Rotterdam that boxer who stayed in the
service when we got study-leave and beat his
chest every morning like Tarzan and then bellowed
"without this strong arm the kingdom is no more
than an appendix"
later on I saw him in a protest march he recognized
me and bellowed just as loud as he used to do
"I don't know if you already know but now I'm a
pacifist"

a cloud
on the wall
of our countenance
and drifts away

no, says Anna Marie it's

now been arranged so that I live
alone with my mother and the memory
they also made me clear about that on
Mallorca that that's true and that that's
good but that doesn't take away from the fact
that I've got to keep vigilant not only about
the legacy of my earlier life in fact even
of my previous life perhaps but very
certainly about the future which is getting
closer and closer because of time you see
which goes on we can't do anything about
that against time and the spirit of the times
we've really got no answer to that one. . .
but fortunately
I know this island
and not only this island
since because it's also a little piece of the world
it's got a lot of the world in it
and to preserve that and keep it pure
since as you know the whole world is threatened
it's one big battle
you might say between crazies among themselves
but what is crazy
my mother cried out last night:
very loud   the body a guide
                                       and where is my number

she never cries out
and certainly not in the night

172

I say mother you had your number
removed
she stands up
which she never does anymore
walks to the cabinet
gets her insurance paper
from it
sees a number and cries out: that wasn't my number
and crying falls asleep
and then I had a terrific laugh
and thought about that one time
in Mallorca
since even tho it's a madhouse
you can also have a good laugh there
when the mother superior told about
the stutterer and the hunchback
who met each other
and the hunchback asked the stutterer
where are you going

and he answered: I-I-'m go--ing t-t-t-t-oo ththe
                              schschool fo....foor st-st-tutterers

said the hunchback: what for
                              you already stutter

asks the stutterer: sssso wha-wha-t're yayou ddddoing

hunchback: I'm going to the photographer

stutterer: ya-you've ggg-ot to wa-wa-watch out
                              thththat y-your hu--hunch ddoesn't
                              co-come on it.

hunchback: why

stutterer: ththe- then the albu--bum ca-c-can't
cccl-close u-up.

no
I think we
won't ever forget it
not the first word
like if you say A you've got to say B
C comes of itself you think
and not the latter either
all those villages
those cities
no
and not the forgotten self
that goes its way and in its remembering
everything changes
even tho the pedestal is empty
the angel having flown away
and not the hands the eyes the hair
and not the intersection
that empty wrist
tho says Marcel rightly
birds, you see
they keep thinking of us
they fly away to other continents
but they always come back to us
that's how birds are
just like people

later Eulalia wrote:

"I read a page every day
José is working Pilar and Victoria
too whether Victoria and Vicente
are going to get married I still don't
know we have very many rabbits and
the chickens are laying fine
it's a shame that you two aren't here
together we could eat plenty
was with José on Ibiza on a visit to
our nephew who was living in
apartment F and I did read that and
did say that now that I can write
I'm going to write you two this
letter and give you my regards and
hope that you both will be coming
back again soon
I enclose a flower because I can't
write a flower"

Amsterdam 1978
Formentera 1979

Notes

p.23   **Craig Strete**: Cherokee Indian poet, writer

p.31   **Eualia and José**: Schierbeek's neighbors on the Spanish Balearic island of Formentera

p.38   **Marcel**: Schierbeek's farmer neighbor in the hamlet of Nogemont, district of Aisne, in northern France

p.41   **one doesn't know**/not for sure/but one does say in our region: /"Life is like a child's undershirt/short and shitty"

p.47   *moraleinfrei* (from Nietsche)

p.53   **San Fernando and Es Caló**: two villages on Formentera

p.54   **Willem Sandberg**: director of Amsterdam's Stedelijk (municipal) Museum of Modern Art, from 1945-63; first director of the Israel Museum

p.72   **the Grebbeberg**: where the Dutch army held of the German army for two days in May 1940, during the invasion

p.74   **Marlène**/with the beautiful legs/is my best girlfriend she hums: / storms/like the stormers/ like Hitler/and Himmler/we take by storm

p.76   **Menno Terbraak**: Dutch essayist of the pre-World war II generation; author of *politicus zonder partij*

p.77   **Lumey**: When William the Silent, "Father of the Netherlands," led the revolt of the seven northern provinces against Spain, Lumey, head

of the Geuzen ("Sea Beggers") led rebel
Calvinists to regain several vital ports

Colijn: Prime Minister of the Netherlands at the
time of the German invasion in May 1940